Offside  in Ecuatina

Copyright © 1990 Cliff Rennie
Reprinted 2003, 2010 and 2011

ISBN 978-1-87167-669-3

Published by
Christian Focus Publications,
Geanies House, Fearn, Tain, Ross-shire
IV20 1TW, Scotland, Great Britain.
www.christianfocus.com
e-mail: info@christianfocus.com

Cover illustration by Jonathan Williams

Cover design by Alister MacInnes

Printed and bound by Nørhaven,
Denmark

Offside in Ecuatina

Cliff Rennie

CF4·K

Contents

The Unexpected Trip

'It's there ... England are one up, with seventeen minutes of the second half gone. This is just the preparation they wanted for the World Cup.'

The excited voice of the Sports Commentator reflected the delight of the English fans. One half of Wembley Stadium heaved with dancing, celebrating thousands, while beyond the halfway line to the far end a gloomy silence descended on the Scottish supporters who had just seen their team go a goal behind the 'auld enemy'.

A smile of relief covered the face of Sam Arnott, manager of the home side. Scotland had been settling better as the second half had progressed. They could have scored at any time, but England had beaten them to it. The match was important to both sides as a last outing before the World Cup finals in Ecuatina, South America. Sam Arnott didn't want to lose this one.

Turning to a close-cropped, gum-chewing youngster on the substitutes bench the England manager said, 'Limber up, Terry, this is your big chance.'

Terry Lindley's eyes brightened. He was a promising young midfield player in the English Second Division who was already attracting the attention of top-class sides in England and Europe. He was anxious to convince Sam Arnott that he was good enough to be included in the World Cup squad.

The intended substitution was spotted by Bill Cheyne, Scotland's manager, who saw instantly the threat it posed to his team. They had already put a lot into the game and to be faced with a fresh pair of lungs at this stage might prove enough to tip the balance of the match against them. Cheyne turned to Kevin Smith to tell him he was going on, but it wasn't Smith his eye fell on. Instead he looked straight into the face of Doug Mackay, the young midfield star from Dalkirk Albion, who had shot to prominence as a match-winner in Albion's recent UEFA Cup triumph.

'Get stripped, son,' said the manager, 'keep a tight reign on Lindley – and tell

Rory Macalpine to push forward.' As the coach held the numbers aloft to attract the referee's attention, Bill Cheyne muttered impatiently to himself, 'I didn't plan to do that. Mackay's only here for a bit of experience.'

But it was done and Mike Crawford, the substituted player, came and sat down wearily beside him. 'That English team is strong, Boss,' panted Crawford. 'I'm glad they're not in our section this summer.'

'So what,' grunted the Manager, 'we've got Brazil the favourites, or had you forgotten?'

Doug Mackay certainly had forgotten about Brazil, and Ecuatina as well for that matter. Here was a moment for him to savour – his first international cap, and an appearance against England at Wembley. He soon found, however, that there was to be no time for day-dreaming. He had barely passed on the manager's instructions to Rory Macalpine, when he had to set off in hot pursuit of Terry Lindley. The English substitute was dribbling the ball into the Scottish penalty area, manoeuvring for a shot at goal, when a timely tackle by Doug knocked the ball away from him to a navy-shirted defender who cleared it into the English half of the field.

Wave after wave of English attacks broke on the ranks of the Scottish defence. Doug Mackay was more than holding his own against Terry Lindley and gradually became sufficiently adventurous to try linking up with his forwards in an attempt to grab the equaliser.

One major problem the Scots faced was the skill of the English defence in operating the offside trap, whereby the Scottish players were caught nearer to the English goal than England's defenders were when the ball came through to them. For most of the game, Scottish attacks had been breaking down on this skilfully worked device.

Doug knew the one sure way of springing this trap. It was for the player in possession to keep the ball and dribble it toward the opponent's goal. But that took a lot of confidence. After all, if you were caught in possession a counter attack could be set up, resulting in the loss of a goal. As Doug saw it, he had to try retaining the ball and running at the English defence. Scotland were a goal down and the offside trap was killing off every other initiative.

Scotland had a throw-in. Doug sprinted down the wing attracting the attention of Neil Young, who sent a prodigious throw-in in his direction. Doug trapped the ball, taking the spin out of it. Then, as Driscoll the English left back tackled, the young Scot pushed the ball ahead, hurdled Driscoll's leg and ran determinedly for goal. The English team funnelled back quickly – but not quickly enough. Doug just kept on running, prodding the ball too far each time for a defender to get it. This was one thing the defence hadn't expected – a strong, confident run that left them stranded far from their own goal.

Now there was only keeper Phil Newman to beat. Looking up, Doug saw Phil advancing to meet him. Shifting his balance he hit the ball with the outside of his left foot. It rose over the keeper's head, but there was just enough spin on it to bring it down in time to slip under the crossbar into the net for the equaliser. Now, it was the turn of the Scottish fans to celebrate. Bill Cheyne was happy too, but still puzzled. He hadn't really intended to put Mackay on, yet he couldn't have made a better substitution. It wasn't just the goal that impressed the manager, but the insight that had led the boy to see this was the only way through the tightly marshalled English defence. Yes, the insight, and the confidence to take on that defence single-handed on his first international appearance. It had almost been like David facing Goliath.

Even as Bill Cheyne was wrestling with these thoughts, Scotland were on the attack again. Doug had linked up with Peter Macdougall on the left wing and was running on to a pass from Pete near the right corner of the English penalty area. Tom Rockhurst, England's captain and central defender hurried to close him down. Running over the ball, Doug made as if to back-heel it to Pete. Rockhurst slowed down and prepared to intercept the pass back. Quick as a flash, Doug moved his foot over the ball and drew it forward. As he sprinted into the box, Rockhurst and his whole defence were caught off balance. Once again, only goalkeeper Newman stood between Scotland and a goal. Phil Newman was crafty and experienced. Coming out quickly he narrowed the angle on goal. Doug must shoot quickly or the chance would be gone. Looking up he clipped the ball smartly off his left foot on to his right. The effect was twofold. In the first place the ball which seemed to be going to the keeper's left suddenly swerved to his right, and secondly, the speed of the movement from one foot to the other added power to the shot. Newman could only look on helplessly as the ball rocketed into the net through the narrow gap between his own right hand and the post.

Scotland were now in the driving seat and the crowd knew it. They only needed to keep possession of the ball until the end of the game to win. The English players had other ideas, however. They had fought hard from the kickoff, too hard to take nothing from the match. Roger Dudley, their skilful midfield player, withstood two strong tackles to force his way into the Scottish penalty area before flighting a good cross for Terry Lindley to head into the net and give England a well-deserved equaliser.

As the teams trooped off the field Sam Arnott sportingly shook hands with Bill Cheyne. 'So that's the Dalkirk boy,' he said. 'Very impressive. You'll be taking him to Ecuatina of course.' Bill Cheyne was caught off guard. He hadn't thought for a moment of including Doug in his World Cup plans. Yet it was the obvious thing to do. Sam Arnott would have done so had the lad been born on the other side of the border.

At that very moment the two men were asked to give a brief television interview. Sam Arnott was given an unreasonably hostile reception. He had planned carefully for the game and his team had played according to plan. To some people, however, anything less than victory is unacceptable. Bill Cheyne was almost forced to state that Doug Mackay would be in the Scottish Squad for Ecuatina, the interviewer being impatient with the manager's repeated answer, 'We will see.'

In the Scottish dressing room morale was great. The team could hardly have had a better send-off to the World Cup than a game like this. It was to Ecuatina the conversation had turned again and again, and especially to the game against Brazil which was regarded as the toughest match the Scots had to play.

One person who kept fairly quiet through all the talk was Doug. He had shared a hotel room with another young player, Alec Ferrier, who had remained on the substitutes' bench for the whole match. The two lads had struck up a friendship.

Alec was particularly impressed by Doug's Christian faith. It wasn't just that Doug believed in God, but that his belief so obviously influenced even the way he played football. Few other young players would have had the confidence to take on an international defence as he had done. Doug radiated confidence, and yet he was modest. Alec noted that he had very little to say about himself, although everyone knew he had turned the game when Scotland had looked beaten.

'You must have a good chance of going to Ecuatina now,'said Alec. 'Are you looking forward to it?'

'I haven't even thought of it,' replied Doug. 'My plans were to have a hill-walking holiday in the Highlands. In any case I'm sure Mr. Cheyne has picked his squad by now. After all some of the best players were intentionally left out of the Wembley match to keep them injury-free for the World Cup.'

Later that evening, however, the Scottish manager took the young Dalkirk Albion player aside and told him, 'I thought you played very well today, and I know you've had a good season with your club. Although I had almost finalised my plans for Ecuatina, I still have a place for an extra midfield player. I'm putting you in the squad. We meet in Glasgow next Thursday and fly out to South America on Friday.'

Doug was surprised, but delighted. He had been thrilled to be chosen for Wembley, but this was far better. Even to be a spectator at the World Cup was tremendous, but to have the chance of playing – well, that was really special.

'I'm very grateful, Mr. Cheyne,' said Doug. 'There's only one thing. I don't play football on Sunday, because it's the Lord's day.'

Bill Cheyne could hardly believe his ears. He was all set to argue when he remembered that, apart from their first match, Scotland were not scheduled to play any other game on a Sunday.

'That's all right, son. We'll respect your views on that subject. Mind you it might be a problem if we reach the final, because it's scheduled for a Sunday.'

There was a twinkle in Bill's eye that said it all – not even the manager believed Scotland would make it. That made Doug sad, for he was sure that Scotland's problem would be lack of confidence rather than lack of class.

President Guachoa

Ecuatina was a beautiful country. As the aircraft carrying the Scottish party flew in over the huge forests and sparkling rivers they were thrilled by the breath-taking scenery. The capital city, Pampalla, where the plane landed was attractively laid out, and the large sports stadium which had been specially built for the World Cup could be seen from the airport.

Ecuatina was not a particularly large country and most of the Cup Ties were to be played in or around Pampalla, the only big city. Indeed, Ecuatina had only won the right to host the World Cup Finals because of the untiring efforts of one man, Antonio Gauchoa, the President of the Ecuatina Football Association.

He had successfully argued that, as other South American countries had received the invitation to host the competition in the past, his country too should receive consideration. He had persuaded local businessmen to invest huge sums of money in building the stadium, extra hotels and other facilities to cater for the thousands of football supporters who would pour into the country from many parts of the world.

As the Scottish party travelled through the streets by coach to their hotel they could see groups of fans from all the competing nations. There was a carnival atmosphere in this city of one and a half million people, most of whom had never seen anything quite like it before. A great cheer went up as the coach passed a group of Scottish supporters who recognised their heroes.

'Let's give them something to remember,' said Bill Cheyne. 'They've done us proud, coming all this way to support us.'

Doug was glad to find he was sharing a room with Ally McTaggart, a midfielder who played in the English League. Ally was reckoned to be the best player Scotland had and Doug looked forward to learning a lot from him. The players had three days light training, getting used to the heat and the rather bumpy playing surfaces, before the opening ceremony took place in the massive World Cup Stadium.

It was a glittering occasion with the flags of all twenty-four nations carried aloft as the teams paraded round the track. Doug was interested to see all the squads, but he took special note of the three countries playing in Scotland's group. These were Algeria, Brazil and Hungary, all skilful, exciting teams who could be counted on to play the sort of attacking football which would thrill the World Cup crowds.

As the parade of nations finished all eyes turned to the podium in the centre of the stadium. Senor Mendez, the President of Ecuatina was introduced and spoke briefly in Spanish, with translations in English and German.

Then Antonio Gauchoa, President of the Ecuatina Football Association, addressed the crowds. Within minutes Doug sensed there was something sinister about the man. He had a tough, rasping voice and a hard, arrogant face. His tone indicated that he was an ambitious man and his words were full of self-praise. Doug was relieved that this man was only Football President of Ecuatina and not Political President. He was glad when the long speech was over.

'What a blether!' mumbled Don Dickson, Scotland's goalie, who was standing near Doug. 'He makes our manager sound positively pleasant.' Bill Cheyne heard the remark and glowered round.

'Dickson, I'll see you later,' he snapped.

'That's worth at least fifty press-ups,' laughed Doug.

The ceremony over, the first match in the competition kicked off. West Germany, the Cup holder, were playing against Nigeria. Doug was impressed by the tactical skill of both sides and especially by the shooting power of Bujong, the Nigerian striker, who scored both his side's goals in the 2-2 draw. There was so much for a young player to learn by watching men of such class.

Scotland's first game was on the Sunday against Algeria. Doug was not selected and was not even expected to attend the game. Instead he went to a church in Pampalla where the service was conducted in Spanish. An interpreter translated the sermon, phrase by phrase, into English. The preacher was talking about Christ's promise to build his church so firmly that the gates of hell would not prevail against it. He spoke of how God deals with our lives to build up our faith and to prepare us for his service, sometimes by bringing us into trying and difficult situations, and sometimes by bringing awkward people across our path. Doug could never have guessed how relevant that sermon was going to be for him there in Ecuatina.

Next day the Scottish camp was shrouded in gloom. Two late goals by the Algerians had sealed a victory their outfield superiority fully deserved. It was a non-training day, so Doug decided to go for a stroll down the main street of Pampalla, which was beautifully decorated for the World Cup. There were finely constructed buildings and busy shops. The long, broad street was filled with traffic which hurried noisily on its way.

Doug had taken his camera with him to snap some of the sights for his album. He was turning to photograph the hotel the squad were staying in, when suddenly he was sent flying and landed on his back. He glanced round to see a young lad in his late teens running down the pavement – carrying his camera.

'Hey, stop him!' called Doug. 'He's stolen my camera.' To his amazement nobody seemed the slightest bit concerned about his loss, so Doug jumped up and set off in pursuit himself. The young thief had a good start, but Doug was faster than the average European tourist and quickly began to gain on him. The boy turned down a side-street, but any hope he had to shaking Doug off was fast disappearing, for the Scot was covering the ground at a tremendous speed.

In a final desperate attempt to shake off his pursuer, the youth ran up a lane. It led into a very old part of the town full of narrow twisty streets. Once in there he would be safe. However, before he had covered the hundred metres that would have secured his escape the thief felt a hand coming down firmly on his shoulder. Doug Mackay was annoyed and it showed on his face.

'Why did you steal my camera?' he asked. 'Thought you could get away with it, did you?' he added.

It was obvious to Doug that the boy spoke no English. He was clearly frightened, and hurriedly handed back Doug's camera. Then, turning quickly, he was gone like a flash into the warren of back streets.

'Hmm! Pampalla's not nearly such a nice place when you see it from this angle,' though Doug. He was just turning to head back to the main street when he heard a voice through a window above his head, on the building he was standing beside. He had heard that voice before and almost without thinking Doug moved towards the slightly open door of the building, a warehouse in the lane. Being careful to keep out of sight he looked in and saw a group of tough sinister-looking men listening intently to one of their number.

'That's Gauchoa,' gasped Doug. 'What's he doing in a place like this? This is hardly the headquarters of the Ecuatina Football Association.'

The man's voice seemed sharper and his face harsher than ever and Doug felt a cold shiver down his spine. Very quickly Doug found out what Gauchoa was doing there, for although the young Scot's Spanish wasn't all it might have been it was sufficient to let him realise that Gauchoa was planning a political coup. He was intending to take over Ecuatina.

'Here we have all the guns we will need,' said the Latin soccer boss, holding a rifle menacingly. 'We have boxes of those here,' he added, patting a pile of boxes stacked beside him. 'Soon Ecuatina will be ours. Soon Mendez will be gone forever.'

There was something about the way he said this that frightened Doug as he listened. The man's voice was as cold as steel. What could Doug do? This was a terrible situation to be in.

Then he remembered the words of another citizen of Ecuatina, the preacher he had heard in church the day before: 'Give thanks in all circumstances'.

It was a quotation from the fifth chapter of First Thessalonians, and the preacher had insisted that God frequently leads us into unusual circumstances because he wants us to serve him and help others there.

Bowing his head Doug prayed quietly: 'Thank you, Lord, for leading me here. I trust you have a purpose and that you'll show me what that purpose is.'

Then suddenly, Doug felt a sharp pain, like a blow, on the back of the head, and everything went black.

KIDNAPPED

How long he lay unconscious, Doug couldn't imagine, but, when he came round, the first thing he was aware of was a throbbing pain in his head. The pain seemed to radiate from the spot on the back of his cranium where he had been hit by a hard, blunt object. Doug moaned with pain as he struggled to remember where he was.

Then, at last, it came back to him. He was the prisoner of President Gauchoa. Sitting bold upright the young Scot made to swing his legs off the grubby bed he was lying on in order to stand up but he was yanked backwards by a chain attached to his left wrist. As far as he could make out the chain was fixed to the leg of the bed.

Doug was a prisoner all right. What time was it? Where was he? What would happen now? Where were Gauchoa and his captors? Did they know who he was? All these questions flashed through his mind with a speed which only served to intensify his headache.

Suddenly Doug heard voices. Some people were coming along the corridor towards the door of his room. For the first time it dawned on Doug that he was alone. Nobody knew he had regained consciousness so as the door opened he closed his eyes and waited.

'He eez still out cold,' said a gruff voice.

'He'll be a lot colder soon,' replied his companion.

'Our Presidente will take no risks. We must seize power soon if we are to take advantage of the growing market. Just as well this man had no photographs of this factory.'

Doug froze as he listened. He knew what the man was getting at. They would want to get rid of him permanently so that he could not alert the authorities and quash the coup. But what was 'the market' the man had referred to? Doug opened his eyes ever so slightly to look at the men who by this time had turned away and were talking about something else.

One was small with a moustache that curled up at the ends, while the other was big, overweight and very scruffy. As he turned to look out the window he revealed to Doug's narrowed eyes a nasty scar. Before Doug's furtive glance could take in any more, he heard the door opening. A number of men came into the room talking tensely and one voice could be heard clearly above the others. It was that of President Gauchoa.

'We must move quickly,' he was saying. 'There is no time to lose. Take our uninvited guest down to the slums. They will take care of him there.'

'Ah, Presidente, I will finish him myself,' interjected Scarface.

'No,' replied Gauchoa angrily. 'It must look like an accident. There must be nothing to trace it back to me, or the cause is lost.'

Gauchoa's voice became more and more high-pitched the angrier he got. As he finished it rose to a crescendo.

'Once we take control of this land of ours we can make it the drug capital of the world. From here we can export heroin, and even crack to every country in the world. Have I not built up a whole network of agents world-wide who can smuggle so successfully that no customs force will ever catch them? But first we must gain power and for that we need the element of surprise and still a little time. If your carelessness takes all this from me, Carlos, I will kill you.'

With that there was a sharp sound like a man's face being slapped, followed by the sound of a grovelling apology by Scarface who was as terrified of Gauchoa as were all the others. He certainly was a wicked man, and Doug's blood ran cold as he heard him speak of heroin and crack. So this was 'the market' and this was the dark purpose behind Gauchoa's successful bid to bring the World Cup to Ecuatina.

Although he was afraid, Doug also felt deep anger that the man could be so cruel and selfish as to plunge people the world over into untold misery just for money. Doug prayed quietly, 'Lord, help me. Keep me safe and help me to alert the authorities in time.'

He had barely finished praying when he opened his eyes slightly and saw on the floor beside him a key. Doug concluded that it was the key for the chain and bracelet that were around his left arm.

He was sure nobody was watching so he stretched out his right hand until it closed over the key. He was just about to retrieve it and conceal it when a boot crunched agonisingly down on his hand.

'So, you are not unconscious after all.' It was Gauchoa. 'Never mind, you soon will be – forever.'

'Not me, Gauchoa,' replied Doug bravely. 'I'm a Christian. For me it will be sudden death – sudden glory.'

The football supremo looked startled. The colour drained from his face. He was just going to ask Doug how he knew his name when the Scot went on, 'What about you? Where will you go when you die? Certainly not heaven with an attitude like yours. You are not better than a murderer or a thief.'

The cruel dark features of the dictator turned scarlet with rage and he drew back his fist to smash into Doug's defenceless face.

'Let me have his, Presidente,' cried Scarface Carlos.

'No!' shouted Gauchoa, recovering himself. 'He goes to the slums. No one must connect us with his disappearance.'

As he emphasized the last word, Gauchoa snarled menacingly, but Doug's fear was being conquered by a determination to face this vile man with the demands of God's law.

'You may think nobody knows what you are doing under the guise of being a football president but God knows every

29

man's heart and one day he will expose you and judge you. There will be no disappearance for you then.'

That was just too much for Gauchoa and he launched himself at Doug, striking him about the head and body. 'Take him out of here before I finish him off myself.'

The President's henchmen removed the chain from Doug's wrist and hurried him out of the building toward a car parked at the rear. The youngster was wondering why things had worked out as they had. If he's managed to pick up the key off the floor he would have been able to release his trapped arm and, given an opportunity, he could have made a break for it. But it wasn't to be.

Doug had learned that when prayers were not answered as he had hoped, he should look for any good thing that happened instead, and he acknowledged to himself that at least Gauchoa had been faced with the truth. God was warning the man before he dealt with him. And deal with him he surely would, of that Doug had no doubt. Prayers weren't always answered as you wanted at the time, but in the end they were always answered the best way.

The car was driven off at speed by Scarface, who could not wait to get to the 'Slums' where he felt sure Doug's fate would be sealed. The man had already built up a jealous hatred of this fearless young foreigner who spoke so forcefully to a man who Scarface himself cringed before. Scarface's enthusiasm proved to be his undoing, however, for as he rounded a corner suddenly he crashed into a bus. Doug could see the crash coming and had braced himself for the impact, but Scarface and his friends were thrown around and shaken up.

In the ensuing confusion, Doug wrenched open the passenger door and dashed for freedom. He quickly found himself on the main street of the city, but his heart sank as he realised he was at the opposite end of the street from the team hotel. It was too far to sprint and he had already seen that passers-by didn't bother to get involved if a chap was in trouble. Doug was just getting ready to dodge into a shop for cover when he heard the sound of singing. Turning round he saw a large group of English football fans celebrating their side's success in their opening game of the competition.

Quietly, Doug joined them, taking off his jacket and carrying it over his arm. A few minutes afterwards he saw a car cruising along on the opposite side of the road. He could just make out the worried features of Antonio Gauchoa, who certainly wouldn't want to have Doug talking too freely about his experiences. To Doug's relief Gauchoa never gave the England fans a second glance.

'These lads have appeared in the nick of time,' thought Doug, a great sense of relief spreading over him. He stayed with the fans until they reached the hotel where he was staying and then slipped inside.

'Where have you been, Mackay?' thundered a voice as Doug walked through the revolving doors. The voice belonged to the Scotland manager Bill Cheyne, but it was filled with such annoyance and irritation that it made the young footballer think of President Gauchoa.

'We're not on a sight-seeing tour of Pampalla,' roared Cheyne, oblivious to the shocked looks of tourists as they retreated hastily out of the line of fire. Bill Cheyne was warming to his theme.

'You're a nuisance, Mackay. I have twenty-one other players to look after and staff members as well. How dare you go wandering off without so as much as a by your leave and just appear six or seven hours later?'

Doug felt deeply ashamed. He knew the manager's anger was the measure of his concern for him. After all, he could have been killed, and the manager and other Scots officials in charge of the party would have been held accountable. Although he was only twenty Doug had found his walk with God had led him along the pathway of adventure on more than one occasion, and he had learned to take rebuke passively and without trying to defend himself or justify what he had done. Yet the truth had to be told, for it affected far more people than Doug himself.

'Mr. Cheyne, I'm really sorry for this trouble, but I was kidnapped, and just managed to escape a few minutes ago.'

This took the wind out of the Scottish manager's sails and he stood with his mouth opening and shutting in amazement. Doug explained in as much detail as possible all that had happened but the expression on Bill Cheyne's face suggested to him that he was not getting through. The manager simply kept looking at his returned fugitive as if heather was sprouting by the minute from his ears.

At last Cheyne snorted, 'Are you trying to make a fool out of me, boy? Do you expect me to believe a far-fetched story like that? Go and get something to eat. Mr. Keir here will look after you. Then come back to see me again at once. You are on a one-man curfew. You do not step outside the door of this hotel without my express permission.'

As he walked away in the direction of the dining-room Doug's heart sank. Here he was with a warning the whole of Ecuatina needed, even the world, and his own manager didn't believe him for a moment.

'Lord, help me,' he prayed. 'Only you can get me out of this tangle. Only you can expose Guachoa.'

FAME AND MISFORTUNE

'Cheer up, son,' said Mr. Keir, the secretary of the Scottish team, as Doug stared gloomily at the salad which filled the plate in front of him. 'Mr. Cheyne's bark is worse than his bite. He was so worried when you disappeared today. This place could be dangerous, you know.'

'I do know,' said Doug, exasperation creeping into his voice. 'Gauchoa is set to take over the country. Here, feel the bump on my head. Do you think I imagined that too.'

Mr. Keir, however, was no more prepared to listen than Bill Cheyne, and for the next two days, Doug could not make anyone listen to his story. He could only pray, which he did frequently in the quiet of his own room. Slowly, but surely, he became less agitated and worried.

A verse he had often read in the Bible began to speak to him in a new way: 'He who believes will not be in a hurry.'

That was it. God's timing in all things was always perfect. It was not Antonio Gauchoa who held the key to unfolding events. No, it was Jesus Christ. Doug could trust him. The right moment to expose Gauchoa would come.

Scotland's second game was against Brazil, the favourites, who had beaten Hungary 3-2, in what had been regarded as the best match of the tournament so far. Bill Cheyne went to bed on the eve of the game wondering what his team selection would be. In the early hours of the morning the manager was awakened by someone shaking his shoulder. It was Peter Keir, grim-faced and weary.

'We've got problems, Bill,' said the secretary.

'Don't tell me. Let me guess,' answered the manager, trying hard to be cheerful. 'We're four down to Brazil. It's half time, and I fell asleep in the first ten minutes of the game!'

We're four down all right. Four of our best players have gone down with food poisoning. The doc's doing his best, but they certainly won't be fit for the match with Brazil.'

'Which ones?' asked Bill Cheyne, his voice quivering with apprehension.

'Reid, Dickson, McWilliams and Gallacher,' replied Peter Keir.

'Oh no!' groaned the manager. 'We're finished. We might as well go home. Why – why did this have to happen to us?' he barked angrily.

'It was the fish,' began the secretary, but he was interrupted firmly by Bill Cheyne.

'Why us? We just can't replace these players. This sort of thing never happens to the big nations – the Brazils, the Germans – only to the likes of us.'

Bill Cheyne couldn't put into words how he felt as he dressed quickly and hurried to the sickroom to encourage the players, all four of whom were feeling thoroughly miserable.

'Imagine,' groaned Derek Reid, 'all this way to be knocked out by a few fish.' The general response to that remark suggested that 'fish' was not the favourite food in the Scottish camp at that moment.

By late afternoon it was obvious that Bill Cheyne would need nearly all his fit players stripped for action. Doug Mackay, who would not normally have been considered for such an important match, was given a place on the bench, from which he watched a frustrating first half, as the Scots struggled bravely to hold the skilful Latin Americans.

At the interval the score was 3-1 for Brazil, with little prospect of improvement. Bill Cheyne strove manfully to lift his men for the remaining forty-five minutes, but he seemed to be fighting a losing battle. Then, his mind went back to Wembley a month before. That day, one player had made an immense difference to the course of the game. Could he do it again?

'Mackay, get stripped,' rapped Cheyne. 'Jim Strang, I want you to come off. You've tried hard, but it's not your kind of game today.'

Doug quietly bowed his head in prayer. He wanted to do his best, for less would be no good for his country – and less was not worthy of his Lord. As the team moved up the tunnel Doug found himself next to Ally McTaggart, his roommate.

'Let's use the whole breadth of the pitch,' said Ally. 'Swing the ball about and press forward all the time. That's the last thing the Brazilians will expect – and it's our only hope of winning.'

Doug agreed with that sentiment. It was too late to defend. In any case that was the kind of approach the Brazilians would want, and they would punish it mercilessly.

The second-half was only minutes old when Ally McTaggart ran on to a clearance by the Scottish goalkeeper. He trapped the ball, sold a clever dummy to his opponent and veered inside toward the centre circle. Looking up he saw Doug running full speed over the halfway line. Ally released the ball at just the right time, a perfectly weighted pass that drifted over the heads of the advancing defence and landed about thirty yards from goal. The Brazilian goalkeeper came off his line smartly, but Doug was careering towards goal at full speed. He reached the ball yards ahead of the keeper and poked it sharply over his outstretched arms into the empty net.

The Brazilians counter-attacked fiercely from the restart. Palto, their brilliant striker beat three defenders in a mazy run that took him within twenty yards of goal, but his final shot was brilliantly tipped over by Bill Hamilton, the substitute Scottish goalie. The resultant corner kick was headed clear by Geordie Neilson, Scotland's central defender.

His clearance came bouncing toward Ally McTaggart who was facing his own goal with two Brazilians at his back.

Because McTaggart had been looking around carefully, before the ball came to him, he knew Doug was about thirty yards behind him, near the centre. Without looking round, he scissors-kicked the ball over his own head, landing on his back in front of the two bewildered Brazilians.

As Doug trapped the ball he heard Martin Skinner, the lanky right-winger, shouting from the touchline. Without looking up Doug swung his left foot at the ball and sent it over the heads of the Brazilian defence, who were becoming extremely nervous of this aerial soccer. Skinner was very fast. Putting his head down he charged towards goal, gathering the ball about twenty-five yards out. The Brazilian keeper remained back within the six-yard box, unwilling to risk the humiliation of losing another race for the ball which might cost his side a goal.

But as Skinner forced his way into the penalty-box the keeper had no option. He rushed towards the advancing forward and threw himself bravely at his feet. With a neat swerve, however, Martin Skinner evaded the challenge and slammed the ball into the net.

The huge Brazilian support was stunned. Their samba drums fell silent and their rhythmic dancing slowed to a halt. They had never expected this. Meanwhile the comparatively small contingent of Scotland fans were celebrating with abandon. The impossible was happening. Even as they tuned their voices to sing, Scotland were mounting yet another attack.

A quick passing movement on the right between McTaggart and Mackay put Doug in the clear right on the edge of the box. In desperation the Brazilian centre-half, Meralldo, up-ended the youngster, who was threatening them every time he got the ball.

Ally McTaggart moved forward to take the free-kick. At the last moment Doug rushed across the front of the goal calling for the ball. It was designed as a decoy run, to pull the defence out of position, and it worked perfectly. Meralldo and one of his big, burly colleagues lumbered across the penalty-box after Doug as McTaggart floated the cross towards big Geordie Neilson whose header beat the keeper to finish up in the corner of the net.

Amidst the scenes of jubilation that followed the goal the Scots didn't notice the Brazilians make a double substitution. Off went the luckless goalie who had lost more goals in one game than most Brazilian keepers lose in five or six matches.

Off too went the Brazilian charged with the thankless task of marking Doug Mackay. They were replaced by two determined looking individuals who sensed they were battling to restore the honour and prestige of Brazil.

Many another team would have crumbled and given up after losing three goals in half-an-hour, but not Brazil. Back they came, and scored the equaliser their efforts deserved. The goal followed a blunder by Doug who, for once, had allowed his concentration to wander, and found himself, in possession of the ball, being forced back toward his own goal. He had waited far too long before making the pass-back his goalkeeper was waiting for, and his new marker, the Brazilian substitute, robbed him of the ball and squared it quickly for Palto to score.

The samba drums revived their arrogant rhythm. They seemed to mock Doug's silly mistake. Scottish heads went down. Was their great effort going to be in vain? A draw might not be enough to enable them to qualify. Indeed they might not even get a draw. Brazil were pressing forward, looking for the goal that would kill off the game and the Scots were missing Ally McTaggart who had been substituted due to exhaustion after his tremendous efforts in the equatorial heat.

Another fierce shot from Palto was firmly held by Bill Hamilton. The keeper quickly threw the ball to one of the fullbacks, who in turn pushed it down the left wing to Doug. A neat body swerve took Doug away from his determined marker and a clever pass put Horace Buchan, Scotland's striker, in the clear.

He tried to take on the defence, but sheer weight of numbers forced him back. Seeing Doug coming up he passed the ball to him. The youngster flicked the ball up with the outside of his left foot without breaking his stride, and used his knee to propel it up to head height. Using his neck muscles to keep the ball bobbing gently on his head he moved steadily toward the Brazilian penalty area.

It has been a second-half full of surprises for the Latin American side but this really took the biscuit. As the defence was trying to tackle Doug and 'untie' the ball from his head, he let it roll down his neck and back. Then, striking it with his heel so that it came up over his head he took a few brisk steps forward and smacked the ball with his left foot. It thundered past the goalkeeper into the corner of the net.

The beat of the samba drums died sharply. The flag of Brazil hung limply in the hands of supporters who knew their team now had no way back, and for the first time the Scots began to believe they could win the World Cup. Doug disappeared from view as happy colleagues engulfed him with their congratulations, for in any circumstances it would have been a spectacular goal, but in a classic cup-tie like this it was remarkable.

After the game, reporters and cameramen from all over the world wanted to speak to Bill Cheyne and Doug. Suddenly, Doug realised this was God's time. This was the moment to expose Gauchoa. Having prayed quietly, Doug began his story, telling how he had been thumped on the head, tied up, threatened with death and how he finally escaped. He repeatedly stressed that Antonio Gauchoa's intention was to usurp power and turn Ecuatina into the centre for drugs trafficking in the world. Doug politely answered questions put to him, some of them pointed and even hostile.

At last it was all over. An astonished silence hung over the interview room. One by one, the reporters left, until only one remained, a young lady. She introduced herself to Bill Cheyne and Doug as Marcia Holman, a reporter for an influential American newspaper.

'You may find this hard to believe,' she began, 'but my newspaper sent me here to investigate allegations of drug-running. I could find absolutely nothing. I don't know why I came to watch the game, partly boredom, I guess, partly to have at least something to report when I get back. But I wouldn't have believed in my wildest dreams that I would unravel a story like this.'

She smiled, 'I'm going to send the story in right away. I'll let you know what happens. I'm staying at the Excelsior Hotel, if you have anything else to tell me.'

Doug assured her that he would let her know if there were any more developments and expressed his gratitude to her. The more people who believed his story and did something about it the better.

By this time Marcia and Doug had emerged from the stadium and were standing on the pavement of a quiet side-street. As Doug began to cross the street to where the team coach was parked Marcia shouted after him.

'You had better be careful. Guachoa knows who you are now, and he will be

45

desperate to get you before you say any more. You're too famous for him to ignore now.'

But Gauchoa had no intention of ignoring Doug. Even as the lad crossed the road a car parked nearby roared into life and sped towards him.

'Look out, Doug!' screamed Marcia.

BEWARE THE WAREHOUSE

Bill Cheyne felt frozen to the spot as he saw the car bearing down on Doug. His mouth opened but no words would come. The intended warning stuck somewhere in the back of his throat.

But Doug had heard Marcia's shout and, seeing the car, he put his head down and ran to the opposite side of the road. Throwing himself the last few yards he landed just in front of the coach, escaping by inches the car that would surely have killed him, and which roared away into the night, leaving two dozen shaken witnesses.

As his team-mates poured out of the coach, Doug struggled to his feet sore and dazed, to hear the voice of Bill Cheyne.

'Son, I'm sorry I didn't believe you. Obviously you were kidnapped and

what you've said about Gauchoa is true.
Whoever was driving that car wanted to
silence you for good.'

'Thanks to Marcia here, I had just
enough warning to make it, but another
second and he would have hit me,' said
Doug, smiling to the young reporter.

Marcia, for her part, could scarcely
talk. She was overwhelmed by what
she had just witnessed, but she was so
relieved Doug was all right. 'Quickly,' she
said, coming to herself, 'we must tell the
police.'

One of the Scottish officials had already
hurried off to a telephone to do exactly
that and soon the police arrived. They
took note of all the appropriate details
and, while two officers remained behind
to take statements from the team and
officials who had seen the incident,
Doug, Marcia and Bill Cheyne were taken
down to headquarters to make further
statements.

Doug's interview after the match
had been flashed round the world
on television and his comments were
of special interest to the police.
Lieutenant Vidal who was in charge
of the investigation listened quietly as
Doug went over his story again.

At last he asked Doug, 'Could you take
us to that warehouse?'

'Yes,' said Doug rising to his feet, 'let's go.'

'No ... no,' interjected the lieutenant with a smile. 'You have had a very eventful evening, enough excitement for one night. We will go in the morning.'

'Good idea,' agreed Bill Cheyne. 'We've no training tomorrow anyway, Doug, and we can go sightseeing in the afternoon.'

'No thanks,' replied Doug with a shudder, 'I've seen enough sights here to keep me going till I get back to Scotland.'

As they left the police headquarters Doug senses he should asked Marcia a question: 'When do you intend to report this to your newspaper?'

'Oh, sometime tomorrow,' she answered, 'after we've been to the warehouse.'

Doug smiled, 'Tomorrow! "Tomorrow never comes!" as somebody once put it. Why not report tonight. I just wish we'd gone to the warehouse tonight.'

'Oh, you're too much!' interrupted Marcia, with a mixture of admiration and irritation. 'You would have us all run off our feet – the Brazilians, the Police, *The Manhattan Echo*...'

'Okay,' conceded Doug. 'As somebody else said, "Rome wasn't built in a day." I just hope they catch Gauchoa soon.'

The next morning as Doug was reading the Bible before going downstairs for breakfast he came to Isaiah 53. The very first words seemed to stand out for him. "Who has believed our message? And to whom has the arm of the Lord been revealed?" The prophet Isaiah had found that, although he had a message that was not only true, but wonderful, in that it was bringing salvation and blessing to all the people, very few were prepared to believe him.

At breakfast the players were still overwhelmed by the events of the previous night. Ally McTaggart was especially inquisitive. 'How did you know it was Guachoa? I can't remember what he looked like, let alone how his voice sounded.'

As Doug explained the impression the soccer supremo had made on him even as he addressed the massed teams during the opening events of the World Cup, Ally sensed that Doug could weigh people up and see through their pretensions in a way that was quite new to him. Was this a God-given insight too?

Their conversation was interrupted by Horace Buchan, who had just joined them at their small table. 'What a place this is!'

said Horace. 'I've tried to phone home, five times this morning, and all I get is the message. 'All lines are engaged' in three different languages. Not only that but the TV. Stations are just showing cartoons and old films. Every so often there's a promise that normal service will be resumed as soon as possible.'

After breakfast Lieutenant Vidal and two officers called for Doug. Marcia had arrived by then and all five went off to visit the warehouse where Doug had been held captive. Doug had a good sense of direction, and soon found the building, but when they entered it his jaw dropped. It had been completely changed.

Gone was all evidence of guns and grenades, instead there were rows of paper sacks piled high on stillages. The clerk in the office was helped by a secretary as he dealt with the business side of things, while two men with fork-lifts were transporting the stillages of sacks to a loading-bay at one end of the warehouse for dispatch throughout the country and abroad.

'This has been completely altered,' said Doug firmly. Lieutenant Vidal looked puzzled.

'Let's have a word with Mr. Santara, the clerk,' he suggested. The two men spoke in Spanish, and Doug could not follow the conversation, but when the clerk began to laugh it was obvious he was dismissing Doug's idea.

Then the young Scot noticed something that jogged his memory. Turning to Lieutenant Vidal, he said, 'Ask him how long Carlos has worked for him.'

Vidal obliged and the clerk replied, 'Two months. He came to join us when we were looking for extra workers.'

'Now ask him how I knew his name was Carlos,' said Doug.

The clerk turned red, for he knew he had been caught out. Doug had recognised the scar on Carlos's face and knew that although he had tidied himself up and was wearing smart overalls he was none other than the man who had been driving Doug to the slums when he had crashed the car.

I'll have a word with him,' stated Vidal, but as the Lieutenant headed purposefully towards him, Scarface Carlos fled, escaping out the back door into the warren of old streets nearby , with the two police officers chasing him.

'What do we do now?' Marcia asked Lieutenant Vidal impatiently. 'It's obvious he is guilty. Whatever they've done here to make things look different, Guachoa and his men are traitors who want to take over the country.'

'It's not as simple as that,' answered Vidal. 'We have no clear proof with which to move. We cannot arrest Senor Gauchoa on the word of one man. If only we could find guns or drugs, or get a confession from Carlos. Remember, if Senor Mackay is correct, then our suspect will be a very angry, frightened and confused man, and before long he will make mistakes.'

'In other words,' interjected Doug, 'Gauchoa was hoping Ecuatina would make it into the final of the Cup so that he could have carried out the coup when the whole nation's attention (and the world's attention) was fastened on the competition. In that way he could pose as the champion of the people, compelled to take power from an uninspiring President.'

'Only now,' added Marcia, her eyes brightening as she saw the pieces of the jigsaw fitting together, 'Gauchoa's plan and intentions have been exposed by Doug and he must abandon them or change them.'

'Yes, exactly,' nodded the Lieutenant, 'and my guess is that if he doesn't act soon, then he will give up the whole idea.'

'He won't,' said Doug firmly. 'Of that I'm certain. He is a fanatic with a thirst for power. He'll try something.'

Lieutenant Vidal's men returned at that point without Carlos. The shrug of their shoulders told it all. They had lost him without trace. Vidal drove Doug and Marcia back to the team hotel where they found Horace Buchan and others nearly frantic with annoyance.

'Those telephone lines are still not working,' complained the striker.

'I'm sure they're working on it,' said Doug with a smile.

But as Horace rushed away to try yet again, Marcia confided in Doug her worst fears.

'No telephones. No television. There's something up here,' she said with concern in her voice. 'After all they've had plenty of activity here for the past two weeks without it affecting the telephones. And to have the television off as well. I'm suspicious Gauchoa's up to something, and if so, that means he has the media and communications people on his side.'

'That's alarming,' said Doug. 'He could blackout news coverage for the whole country just long enough to mount his attack. In fact that means he must plan to make his move soon.'

'Yes, I'm glad I took your advice,' said Marcia.

'What advice?'

'About telephoning the story to the *Echo* last night instead of waiting until today. Our editor thinks it's a marvellous story. He's going to keep in touch with Washington because of the implications of it all. He says he hopes to meet you one day. I'm glad I met you too. This is the story of a lifetime, and I've never had so much adventure before.'

Doug was silent. He was straining to make out a sound he could only barely hear. Moving to the door of the hotel he looked upwards.

'Just as I thought – helicopters, and by the look of the camouflage on them they're military helicopters.'

'Isn't that President Mendez' residence they're circling over?' asked Marcia. They she added, 'You ... you don't think the coup is actually taking place, do you?'

As if to answer Marcia's question an army land-rover was speeding up the busy main street.

'Get inside,' said Doug, taking her by the arm.

'But this could be the greatest story I will ever cover,' protested Marcia.

'Or the last,' answered Doug grimly. 'If Gauchoa is in this it will not be a bloodless coup. Some people will probably get hurt, maybe even killed. Believe it or not you and I are prime targets.'

'Gauchoa wouldn't dare hurt me; I'm an American citizen,' argued Marcia pompously.

'You're right, of course,' said Doug with a smile. 'Gauchoa won't touch you – he'll send you to the slums instead.'

Marcia shivered at the very mention of the word. What unimaginable horrors lay there behind those small back streets of Pampalla. Quickly she followed Doug.

'Where are we going?' she asked nervously.

'I'm going to look for a couple of uniforms.'

'What? What sort of uniforms? Surely this isn't the time to look for uniforms?'

Doug, however, had already disappeared into the servants' quarters from which he reappeared a few minutes later carrying some clothes.

'Quick!' he said to the astonished Marcia. 'Put these on.' Then he disappeared in the direction of his room.

Finding a ladies' room the young American girl put on the uniform of a maid, hoping the funny headdress disguised her distinctive hairstyle. When she came out into the foyer of the hotel, she gulped to see four or five army officers.

Two of them were talking to Bill Cheyne who was gesticulating frantically in an attempt to convince the soldiers that he could not gather the Scottish squad together.

'No training today,' he was saying. 'Sight seeing.' He even held his hands up to his eyes like binoculars to emphasise the word 'sightseeing'.

The remaining officers were hurrying around from foyer to lounge, from room to room, obviously looking for someone. She suspected the subject of their search was Doug, an opinion confirmed when she heard the officer in charge asking Bill Cheyne.

'Where eez Senor Mackay?'

'Doug?' replied Cheyne, 'Oh, he was with Lieutenant Vidal this morning. You should telephone police headquarters.'

The officer shook his head. 'He is not there,' he replied. 'It is important we find him – for his own good.'

The men did not leave until they had searched the hotel and when they did finally withdraw they looked angry and perplexed.

Marcia's sense of adventure was becoming a little frayed at the edges as she realised the dangers she faced, for as Gauchoa's net closed in on Doug it was closing in on her too. She was wondering what to do next when a waiter approached her, asking something in Spanish. She panicked. What had he said? Now, she would be found out. What would happen to her?

THE SECRET PASSAGE

The seconds seemed like hours as Marcia tried to think what to say. Why did this waiter have to ask her a question just at that moment? She was all set to blurt out that she couldn't speak Spanish very well when the waiter spoke again, this time in a funny Scottish accent.

'Oh, you!' said Marcia in a mixture of exasperation and relief.

'We'd better get moving,' whispered Doug. 'In five minutes the servants change over as the new shift comes on duty. We'll need to put their clothes back, but we'll also need to borrow other clothes so that we aren't too easily recognised outside. I'll see what I can do. Meantime, return the maid's uniform and meet me here in twenty minutes.'

Doug found Bill Cheyne and explained that he and Marcia would need to leave and try to escape across the border fifty miles to the north. He didn't need to impress on Bill how serious things were. The television news programme was carrying the full story of the coup. Gauchoa was being hailed as the man to meet 'the needs of the hour', a President who would bring great wealth into the country. Viewers were assured that the World Cup would not be affected in any way by the sudden turn of events.

Bill Cheyne found some warm clothing for Doug without difficulty; but for Marcia it was more of a problem, Mrs. Keir finally coming to the rescue with a pair of trousers and an anorak.

'We'll have a good meal before we go, Marcia,' said Doug. 'We might have to walk most of the night to get over the border.'

As they were finishing their meal, Bill Cheyne came with the news that there was an armed guard on the front door. However, his own room was on the first floor at the back of the hotel. He had checked and there was no guard there. By tying a few sheets together two or three team members could lower Doug and Marcia to safety.

'You must hurry,' said Bill Cheyne, 'in case Gauchoa's men return.'

'Yes, but before we go, I'm, going to pray. We will need God's help if we're going to make it safely out of the country.'

So saying, Doug prayed for God's protection not only for Marcia and himself, but also for the whole Scottish team, and for the nation of Ecuatina. He prayed God would bring the wicked drugs' baron to justice and protect innocent people from the iniquitous trade.

His prayer at an end, Doug shook hands with Bill Cheyne and began his climb out of the first-storey window. Marcia quickly followed him. By the time Bill had pulled the knotted sheets back through his room window the gallant pair had disappeared into the night.

They threaded their way carefully through the lanes and back streets that lay behind the main street. They kept heading north and within half an hour they were near the perimeter of the town. Just as they were beginning to relax, however, Marcia heard a sound.

'What's that?' she said.

'What's what?' asked Doug.

'Listen! There it is again. Somebody's crying.'

'It's coming from behind that wall,' said Marcia. Looking over the wall Doug shone the flashlight in the direction of the sobbing. It illuminated a woman who immediately cringed away crying and moaning, until Marcia's gentle voice soothed her fears.

'Don't be afraid. We won't hurt you. We're on the run ourselves. You can come with us if you want to.'

The woman could only speak a little English and found great difficulty controlling her trembling voice, but at last the two friends grasped that she had been a servant in President Mendez' home. That afternoon rebel troops, supporters of Gauchoa, had surrounded the house and were holding the President captive. The woman, whose name was Isabella, liked President Mendez.

'We all like him,' she said. 'He rules our country well.' But it was when she spoke of the Mendez children that Isabella became particularly emotional. They were called Edouard and Helena, and they, along with their mother, had been most upset by the coup. Isabella had managed to escape by means of a secret passage leading from the study to the rear of the courtyard. She had kept running until she could run no more and collapsed behind the wall where they now found her.

'I have prayed that I would find someone who could help our beloved President and now you have come along. Please will you help us?'

Doug was already forming a plan in his mind. As there was a secret passage into the President's home, it might be possible to rescue him and his family. They would need to know as much as possible about the layout of the house and where members of the family might be held. It wouldn't be easy but with Isabella's help it could be done.

Isabella was delighted when she heard Doug and Marcia were willing to come back with her and she brought them quickly and quietly to a field from which they could get to the back of the courtyard, and the secret passage.

They crouched behind an old disused barn until all was clear, then they made their way rapidly but silently to a hidden door, almost covered over with ivy. This opened to reveal the narrow passageway Isabella had spoken about. They could only advance along the passage slowly, one at a time.

Isabella led the way and after a few minutes they reached a secret doorway which opened into a large room which was in fact the study. Now they came to the difficult part. The Mendez family would be closely guarded. Somehow they had to distract the guards long enough to rescue the children and their parents.

Doug explained his plan slowly and patiently to Isabella whose eyes lit up as she listened. She rummaged in the desk, knowing her way expertly about the study, even in the dark.

'Ah!' she grunted with satisfaction, taking a cigarette-lighter from the drawer and handing it to Doug. He rubbed the wheel of the lighter, producing a rich, steady flame which would serve his purpose adequately.

Isabella handed him the small wastepaper basket from under the desk and he made his way back to the secret passage. As he entered it and made his way to the rear of the courtyard, Marcia came after him a little way.

'Doug,' she said quietly. 'Don't you think you should pray again. This is very dangerous.' He thought for a moment before answering.

'You pray,' he answered. 'That will be a real encouragement for me.'

Marcia was quiet. Although she had been brought up in a religious home and believed in God, her idea of prayer had always been very limited. Only in very special circumstances had she even looked for an answer.

'I... I don't know how to pray,' she said. Marcia was hanging her head and feeling close to tears.

'Do you believe God is able to hear you?' asked Doug.

'Yes – yes, I do,' she answered with growing conviction.

'Then talk to him and tell him all about your problem and ask for his help.'

Marcia gulped, then started to pray. 'Dear God, I'm sorry I don't pray nearly often enough. Please help me to trust you more, even as Doug does. Look after him and keep him safe. Oh, God, this is very dangerous. Help Isabella to find the Mendez family and bring them to the study, so that we can escape. Lead me to become a ... better Christian. Amen.' As she finished Marcia sighed with relief.

'How did I do?' she asked, waiting a little nervously for Doug's verdict. 'Doug?'

But no answer came, for Doug was already slipping out of the hidden doorway to make his way across the field.

'Oh!' grumbled Marcia with exasperation. 'That is the most maddening individual.' Yet, secretly, she almost appreciated his departure at that moment. In his own quiet way Doug had been saying, 'Look, Marcia, you don't need my verdict on your prayers. God is happy with them and that's all that counts.'

Though danger, and even death, stalked their very footsteps Marcia felt a warm happiness she'd never experienced before. God loved her too.

Presently, as Isabella and Marcia watched from the study window they saw flames begin to rise from the old barn. Very quickly it was ablaze and the air was filled with the shouts of both servants and rebel soldiers as they ran to and fro with buckets of water.

Marcia touched Isabella's arm. 'Now,' she said, 'better go now.'

Peeking round the study door Isabella saw there was no-one in sight. Quickly she ran upstairs where intuition told her the family would be held under guard. She hesitated a moment, then, remembering the fire extinguisher which hung on the wall nearby, she went over and lifted it from the bracket which was securing it. She tiptoed to the door and listened carefully. She could hear the excited voices of the children, as they saw the flames leaping into the sky. The surly guards were reprimanding them.

Taking a few steps back, Isabella ran to the door crying, 'Fuego, feugo!' She banged on the door, then flung it open, to the astonishment and anger of the guards. In Spanish she told them they must hurry downstairs and help with the fire. Without pausing to argue she dumped the fire extinguisher in the hands of the bigger guard and turning on her heels she ran down the stairs, leaving the guards protesting behind her.

As Doug had anticipated, the suddenness of it all threw the guards into a panic. Without thinking they ran down the stairs, leaving the bedroom door unlocked. Isabella had ducked into a broom cupboard on the stairway. She saw the men disappear on their way outside and she hurried back up to the children's room. Isabella had been delighted to notice not only Edouard and Helena in the room, but also their parents. Now the whole family was left unguarded.

When she opened the door Isabella was greeted with mingled tears and cries of joy. She embraced Senora Mendez and the children in turn and then led them quickly and quietly down to the study, where Marcia was waiting for them. Soon Doug arrived to say that the way was clear for them to escape. He led them down the secret passage to the hidden door from which a furtive glance yielded the information that all hands were preoccupied with the blazing ruin.

'I always hoped that old barn would come in useful one day,' said Senor Mendez, 'but I never dreamt it would save my life.' Then he motioned to Doug. 'Over this way,' he said. 'I have a car which will help us to escape.'

The car was in a garage which was unlocked and Senor Mendez had a spare key hidden on a shelf. He opened the car and shepherded his wife and children together with Marcia into the back. Letting the handbrake off, Senor Mendez helped Doug push the car quietly out of the garage and down the driveway to the front gate.

All at once Doug's heart sank, for at the gate two guards could be seen. They could hardly be unaware of the fire, yet they had been too experienced to leave their post. Doug bowed his head in quiet prayer. At any moment these men might turn and see the car that was going to bear their captives to freedom. As he thrust his hand into pocket he felt the lighter.

Suddenly it came to Doug. Another fire! This time at the perimeter fence. If he could distract the guards the family might just manage to escape. Having quickly shared his plan with

Senor Mendez, Doug crept stealthily across the lawn till he came to the far corner of the garden. There was some dry grass just beyond the railings, which would flare up quickly without causing damage to the greener vegetation inside the garden.

Reaching out carefully Doug sparked the cigarette lighter into life. The flame licked the dry grass which began to crackle. Doug hurried back, towards the gate dodging from tree to tree. By the time he had arrived at the gate the guards had noticed the fire and were hurrying to investigate. Doug swung the large gates open for Senor Mendez to drive through. Then, closing the dates, he jumped into the passenger seat. As they drove quietly off they couldn't see the guards who were still out of sight fighting the small fire. Doug sighed with relief. The fact that Gauchoa's men hadn't missed the Mendez family gave them extra time to escape.

Senor Mendez knew the back roads from Pampalla to the northern border and, although the journey took longer, they were able to avoid roadblocks or spot checks by rebel soldiers. Senor Mendez was very grateful to Doug for all he had done both for him and for Ecuatina.

'I can tell you,' he said, 'your disclosures on television forced Guachoa's hand. He would not have tried to seize power probably until the day of the World Cup Final, by which time all his plans would have come to fruition. You have warned our people and the world, and the troops and police who are loyal to me are getting ready to strike back. Gauchoa will be a worried man tonight.'

Soon they reached a quiet lane where Senor Mendez stopped the car. 'We can drive no further,' he said, 'but if we follow this path we will come to the house of a loyal friend of mine who will help us to get across the border.'

Doug was glad to know their journey was coming to an end, for all the running from place to place, together with the tension of so many narrow escapes, was beginning to wear him out.

The Mendez family were welcomed with passionate tears of mingled joy and sadness by Juan Pedro and his wife who lived in the remote house. It was obvious to Doug that the ordinary people of Ecuatina (the ones who really mattered) cared deeply for their President.

Introductions made and greetings exchanged, the travellers sat down for a welcome meal. Juan Pedro did not have much to set before his guests, but the chicken and sweet potatoes served by Senora Pedro were devoured with obvious gratitude.

The meal over, they were just beginning to relax when they heard three loud raps on the door. Juan Pedro stiffened with obvious fear. He looked across the table at the President questioningly, but a shrug of the shoulders indicated Senor Mendez had no idea who the late caller was. Even as they watched, the door opened slowly to reveal two well-built men in sports clothes. It wasn't their clothes, however, which commanded the attention of the occupants, it was the fact that each man held in his hand a menacing revolver.

SWEET AND SORE

Advancing into the room the men looked around the company, weighing up each person carefully.

'Is there anyone else in the house?' asked one of them. Doug noticed he spoke with a pronounced American drawl.

'There are only the children asleep upstairs,' answered Juan Pedro.

The American then addressed Marcia. 'You are Miss Holman of *The Manhattan Echo*; is that correct?'

'Yes, I am and you are from American Intelligence.' The two men looked surprised.

'How do you know that, Miss?' asked the spokesman.

'Because ... because, I've been praying God would guide you to meet us. I knew my editor would be in touch with Washington as soon as I told him the seriousness of Gauchoa's plot. I've expected someone from Intelligence to be sent here to Ecuatina.'

Marcia introduced the Mendez family and Doug to the men from the Intelligence Service, filling them in on the various details of what had taken place. Doug was very impressed by her memory for details, as well as her obvious concern for the people of Ecuatina and her passion for justice.

The Americans introduced themselves as Troy, who came from Texas, and Jack, whose hometown was Chicago. They had crossed the border that evening under cover of darkness and had been standing in a nearby lane planning their next move when they heard the approach of a car.

Hiding in the bushes they had seen Marcia, Doug and the Mendez family leave the vehicle and make the last part of their journey on foot. Such was their training that even in the brief moments of visibility from the car lights they were pretty sure they recognised Marcia from the description given them by the editor of the *Echo*.

The men were certainly impressed by the way they had met up with those they were searching for, but whether or not they saw it as being more than coincidence Doug couldn't tell. Troy and Jack were anxious to get Senor Mendez and his family safely across the border until the conflict was over.

Their sources told them that to the south and east of Pampalla gun battles were raging as forces loyal to the President were resisting the coup. So far the rebels had done no more in the north and west than seize control of the border customs posts. They had almost certainly been planning to kill the President to quell opposition to the coup, and now that he had escaped there would be panic in Gauchoa's ranks.

'We must cross the border tonight,' said Troy. 'There you will find political asylum and perhaps even support. Other countries in South America are very concerned about the possibility of deadly drugs becoming available here in Ecuatina which, up until now, has been a stable country.'

Senor Mendez thanked Doug and Marcia for their help and, accompanied by Isabella, the Mendez family set off with Troy and Jack through the night on a twenty-five mile hike which would take them over the border to a friendly capital where they would find rest and shelter. Edouard and Helena were enjoying this particular journey, for each was being carried on the back of a brawny American.

In the days that followed, Doug and Marcia waited for the return of Troy and Jack. Although they had asked Marcia to accompany them she wanted to stay behind, especially when she knew the Intelligence men wanted Doug to accompany them on a mission which involved uncovering the rebel headquarters the young Scot had stumbled on.

It was frustrating to have to wait and feel so helpless. To make matters worse Doug heard on Juan Pedro's radio that Scotland had lost 1-0 to Hungary, and had finished in third place, ahead of Algeria on goal difference. In fact they just qualified for the second round by the narrowest of margins and were drawn against Ecuatina who had won their own section convincingly.

It was something else, however, that was frustrating Doug most of all – a growing awareness of how much Marcia meant to him. It wasn't just that she was a pretty girl, with a friendly, considerate manner, for those things alone would have made her attractive without generating these emotional problems he was now feeling. The fact was that for fully two weeks he had seen Marcia almost every day.

Furthermore, this was no mutual acquaintance developing slowly and normally in a predictable situation. They had lived with their hearts in their mouths every day. Doug had twice been close to death and Marcia was finding out how dangerous a reporter's life could be. These complex and trying circumstances had deepened their sense of friendship and mutual dependence.

Doug would have missed Marcia if she had gone with the Mendez family, but she too would have missed him. He could not forget the way she had turned and looked at him when the suggestion had been made that she leave. It was more than the reporter's urge for a good story that kept her in Ecuatina.

Ironically, the biggest problem of all for Doug was Marcia's faith. He had seen the new brightness in her eyes during those days in which she had learned to pray with real faith. She wasn't a lady to do anything by halves and her desire to know about God and increase in faith led her to pump Doug with endless questions for, as she constantly reminded him, 'You started me on this journey of faith.'

Had Marcia been a girl who had no interest in Christian things and little belief in prayer, she would have held absolutely no attraction for Doug, who knew that, as a Christian, he would be disobeying God to marry such a girl, or even to become emotionally involved with her.

As Doug had read the Bible, particularly the passages relating to marriage, he had seen that whether or not he was to be married was an important part of God's purpose for his life. If he was to marry, his wife would need to be a Christian, a girl who would share his faith. Doug saw how perfectly his mother complemented his father in the work of the ministry, and he sensed that was what marriage was meant to be, two people sharing a faith and a calling from God together in love. It was not enough that you felt attracted to a girl, she had to be the right one, for surely there could only be *one* right girl.

This was what concerned Doug. Marcia had probably been converted during these dramatic days. If not, she was surely on the way to a living faith. But was she the right person for Doug? Were they compatible, this vivacious, adventure-seeking American and the Scot who, in the last year had seen and suffered enough adventure, tension and danger to last him a lifetime? Anyway, how could he know if Marcia would fit into God's purpose for his life, when he didn't know himself what that purpose was to be.

Yet there she was, day after day, as large as life and growing sweeter with every conversation and dearer with every flowering of her new-found faith. One thing Doug was learning, sore as this turmoil was, it wasn't going to disappear.

Then, one evening as he was praying before going to sleep, it came to him that, just as with so many other challenging experiences, God was wanting him to face up to this, not to run away from it. Why, he did not know. How, he did not know, except that as he looked to the Lord his own faith would be deepened.

As he came to see things from this angle, he became aware to his shame, that he had been resenting Marcia for throwing him into this turmoil. Now he found himself praying for her, with tears, even as a little sister in Christ who needed God's protection through the emotional turmoil she was also unquestionably experiencing. He had seen her eyes almost peering into his soul and mistakenly regarded her as threatening his freedom and disturbing his peace.

Now, he saw that she was wanting reassurance as a young Christian and also wanting help with her awakened feelings. Doug resolved to talk gently but plainly with Marcia next morning and drifted off to sleep with a smile on his lips as the thought stole across his weary brain, 'Boy, I sure hope beating the Ecuatina defence isn't as complex and difficult as this.'

Next morning Doug prayed before going down to breakfast. One of the Bible passages he read was from James 1:19: 'Everyone should be quick to listen, slow to speak, slow to become angry.'

Doug prayed he would have a good opportunity to talk with Marcia, and it came just after breakfast. They had cleared up the dishes and were having a walk in the tree-lined lane near the house. Doug found it easier to talk as they walked along because he did not have to look into those piercing, questioning eyes.

'What do you hope to do in the future, Marcia?' he asked, to which she replied that she wasn't too sure, but couldn't see herself being a reporter for ever; an editor, it was a good job, but now the way she felt, it would maybe need to be something else.

'I know what you're going to be,' she volunteered, which surprised Doug since he did not know himself. 'You're going to be a preacher. That must be a fantastic life.'

Doug groaned inwardly. This conversation was running away from him, like a football match where the other team always seemed to get the break of the ball.

Clearing his throat he began. 'Being a preacher's all very well, if that's what God is calling you to do, but I'm not at all sure that's what I'm called to.' He was trying to be serious, but sensed acutely that he was beginning to sound like a pompous ass.

Marcia smiled, 'Well, you sure can't go on playing football all your life.'

'Anyway,' said Doug, trying again to make his point, 'when we give our lives to God, everything belongs to him. He has a plan for us which involves our career, the places we'll go, the person we'll marry, everything. What we have to do is just obey God faithfully from day to day as he leads us and then, at different times in the future, when we are fully prepared, he'll give us whatever is right.'

Doug waited to see what impression his words had made on Marcia. It had been much harder speaking to her than he had expected.

'It's great to know God won't let us make mistakes in these big decisions of life. We can trust him completely,' she observed.

For a young Christian Marcia's words were full of wisdom and Doug would have been wise to have discreetly changed the subject at that point, but for once he was not trusting the situation into God's hands. He was determined to impress upon Marcia that she was too young a Christian to be even considering marriage.

'You have a lot to learn, Marcia, and a long way to go on the Christian pathway before you are ready to make a serious decision about marriage. So have I. We're both far too young.'

Doug broke off in dismay as Marcia burst into tears. He stammered a sort of apology, but she was already running toward the house, leaving Doug feeling like a heel. He really liked Marcia but he had been afraid lest their feelings for each other became a hindrance to them in their Christian lives.

Sitting down on a stone Doug was conscious of two things. In the first place, he felt worse than ever. To be deeply attracted to Marcia was bad enough, to have hurt her was terrible. How would he face her?

Secondly, he was becoming uncomfortably aware that he had not been as prayerful as he should have been. He had forgotten God's Word and had been far too quick to talk. He committed the situation to God, 'Lord, please work it all out. You understand us both. You know that even if I made a mistake I did it with the best of intentions. Bless Marcia, and lead her safely in the way you want her to go.'

That evening Troy and Jack returned with the news that the Mendez family were safely across the border. International condemnation of Gauchoa's coup was growing. Inside Ecuatina loyal troops were planning a counter-offensive.

'It might help if we could find that arms dump in the warehouse that you were in, Doug,' said Troy. 'If they had a lot of weapons there, it wouldn't be easy to move them all. When you went back with that police lieutenant the weapons were probably still in the building, but cleverly concealed.'

'Probably it was the lieutenant that tipped them off and kept you waiting the next day, when you wanted to return to the warehouse that night,' added Jack. 'Gauchoa must have had some people in high places to try to pull something like this off.'

'But why?' asked Doug in exasperation. 'Why oppose a good man like Mendez and support a crook like Gauchoa?'

'Ah, Doug, not all men are good,' replied Troy. 'Where there's money or power to be had, you will always find men who will stoop to wickedness.'

'Will you lead us back to the warehouse?' Jack asked Doug.

'Certainly,' he replied. 'Anything to put an end to this rebellion.'

They looked in the direction of Marcia who was sitting with Senora Pedro in the kitchen, some ten yards away.

'She would be better to stay here. Things might get tough. It's no place for a pretty girl,' reasoned Troy.

'But who is going to tell her,' asked Jack. 'It will need to be somebody who is good at getting through to her, for she's a fairly determined young miss.'

Slowly they both turned and looked at Doug.

MOUNTAIN OF MISERY

Marcia Holman was feeling very sad as she sat at the kitchen table watching Senora Pedro baking for her family and guests. Thanks to gifts of money from the American Intelligence men, the cheerful South American mother had managed to buy some choice extras and was able to show off her baking skills. Not that Marcia was paying too much attention at that moment, lost as she was in her thoughts.

As long as she could remember life had been a struggle for Marcia. Both her parents had been career people who had set high standards of attainment for themselves in business and both had been successful – at a price. The price, Marcia recalled, had been paid by her in the long hours of family togetherness she had somehow missed out on.

There had been happy moments – father's cuddles and mother's kisses – but they had been all too few and far between because happiness takes time, and career parents don't always have time. If she wanted extra affection a clever girl could always earn it by working hard, getting good grades in school, impressing the neighbours and relations. It meant a lot for her ambitious parents that Marcia was a 'good girl', but she had grown up with a sense of deprivation. She envied Juan Pedro's little daughter, a messy six year old whose childhood seemed to be one long delightful trip of outsmarting her older brother and 'mothering' her little brother. These children were expected to enjoy their childhood and Marcia knew that was how it should have been for her.

But it was not her parents the young American was thinking about at that moment. She was too keenly aware of disappointment from another quarter. Marcia had never met anyone like Doug Mackay. It wasn't that he was a strong dominating personality, on the contrary he was quiet and unselfconscious with a gentle sense of humour. The thing that had really impressed Marcia was his confidence in God – a confidence that made him brave in the face of danger and cheerful when things looked bleak.

She was drawn to this boy as a struggling swimmer is drawn to a beach rescue. He was an island of assurance in a sea of doubt and she found it easy to have faith when he was around, for his faith in God was so real and natural. Without flattering her in any way Doug had given Marcia the assurance that she was an important person to God. In all her twenty-one years she had never felt so good.

Then her dream had been cruelly shattered by none other than Doug himself. Marcia couldn't remember all he'd said, but she had been rejected yet again, and the old insecurities of childhood were stealing through the corridors of her life to haunt her again. If only she had never met this fellow Mackay. Only one thing comforted her in her misery – her faith in Christ was increasing. Something real had happened in her heart and no disappointment on earth could take it away. She remembered the words of Psalm 73 which Doug had taught her: "Whom have I in heaven but you? And earth has nothing that I desire besides you. My flesh and my heart may fail, but God is the strength of my heart and my portion for ever."

Marcia's eyes filled with tears, but they were tears of gratitude to God who loved her for herself and who would yet strengthen her to withstand any hurt that others could do to her, be it deliberate or unintentional.

She barely felt the hand which gently patted her arm, but she turned at the mention of her name to look into the pain-filled eyes of Doug. She had never seen him look so youthful and helpless before. There was little of the calm resolute power that had always impressed her. Marcia knew instantly that he regretted deeply the hurt he had caused her. Obviously this man could not be at peace when she was so unhappy.

'Marcia, I'm sorry for speaking as I did,' he said, 'I sort of wished I'd kept quiet.'

He was plainly struggling for words and Marcia found herself taking his hand and telling him not to be upset. She was still confused, but now she realised Doug had not been rejecting her at all, he had only been warning her that both of them needed to seek God's will for their lives, and not just drift on into a friendship that might hurt them both in the end. He had spoken as he did out of love, and she appreciated him doing that.

'Marcia, I'm going off with the men after dark to look for the warehouse.' Doug sounded almost apologetic.

'Great,' she smiled, 'I can't wait to see what's hidden there. Do you think we'll find weapons?'

'It could be quite dangerous,' he replied.

'Don't worry, Scottie,' she answered, 'I'll look after you.'

Doug opened his mouth to argue, but as he saw the mischievous glint in her eye, he knew there was little point. Instead he smiled sheepishly and turned back to break the news to Troy and Jack.

That evening the four of them drove down to Pampalla in a car Troy and Jack had brought over the border with them. They used the back roads and were able to get close to the city without being stopped by rebel soldiers. They parked in a suburb and made their way carefully, avoiding the main streets, to the warehouse, which was not as hard to find as Doug had at first feared it would be.

There was no sign of anyone on guard as they tried the door at which Doug had first overheard Guachoa's plans to take over the country. Gently Troy edged the sliding-door open and led the way inside. Hardly daring to breathe, the four followed the path of Troy's flashlight, picking their way carefully round the stacked paper sacks and between the pillars which supported the roof. They examined the various stillages, but could find nothing.

'Are you sure this is the place, Doug?' asked Jack.

'No question,' replied Doug, 'and we are more or less at the place where the guns were hidden.'

'Over here,' interrupted Marcia. 'Bring the light over here.'

In the darkness she had stumbled against one of the stillages and kicked the bottom layer of sacks, causing it to tear. She had heard a sound like sugar pouring out. Stooping down she had taken a handful of powder off the floor.

'I don't know what this is,' she said excitedly, 'but I don't think it's for baking with.'

The light revealed a white powder-like substance. Troy dipped his finger in it and tasted it.

'Heroin,' he said in a voice full of concern.

'Just as I thought,' announced Marcia firmly. 'It's just as well I came along or you might have searched all night and never found it.'

Doug couldn't quite understand why these words were addressed to him.

'There's enough of the stuff here to poison the whole countryside,' gasped Jack.

'What are we going to do?' asked Marcia excitedly.

'There's only one thing we can do,' answered Troy, taking a small bag of heroin from the sack. 'We must get this dope to our superintendent. He's waiting just across the border. President Mendez will help him get in touch with the loyal police chiefs who can make a planned swoop on the warehouse and expose this mountain of misery.'

'But that could take hours. Gauchoa's men could destroy the evidence by that time,' moaned Marcia with exasperation. 'Can't we just go straight to the police?'

'That could be the worst thing to do,' countered Jack. 'If we went to the wrong officers not only would they arrest us and tip off Guachoa, they would see to it the message never got through to our superintendent. Better to take a little longer and be sure we get it right.'

'Marcia's right about one thing,' said Troy. 'Gauchoa's men could come back at any time. If they did try to move any of this junk we would want to know where they had put it. Doug, would you stay here and keep an eye on things? Hopefully, nobody will come, but you never know.

If all goes according to plan the police should get here by the early hours of tomorrow morning.'

Doug agreed to stay. He hoped he had succeeded in concealing his reluctance, for he still remembered his previous meeting with the rebel gang in that very same warehouse when he had only narrowly escaped death.

'I'll stay with Doug,' volunteered Marcia.

Doug's heart sank. It was bad enough having to keep watch over the warehouse without having to keep an eye on this intrepid reporter. He was just beginning to protest about the idea, when Troy accepted Marcia's offer.

'Good. I'll leave this flashlight with you. Don't take any chances. Don't tackle them yourselves. These men are very dangerous.'

'Yes,' replied Doug weakly, 'they are a bit ruthless. Do you really think it's safe to leave Marcia here?'

But Troy and Jack were already on their way out of the warehouse. Sliding back the large door quietly they crept along by the wall until, under cover of the dimly lit back streets, they could make their way to the car which would take them to their superintendent and President Mendez. Now, at last, the net was tightening around Guachoa.

Doug and Marcia decided to search the warehouse. It was difficult to see very much by the light of the torch, but after searching for more than an hour they made a breathtaking discovery. Beneath a pile of waste paper, which was leaning against a wall, they found a trap-door. Pulling it up they were amazed to find an arsenal of weapons and ammunition that could have equipped a small army. The underground cavity was at least twenty metres square, and it was packed.

'This is grim,' said Doug. 'Gauchoa's rebellion could drag on for months with all this lot.'

'And those drugs,' added Marcia. 'If these get into the wrong hands the suffering will be immense. Doug, let's pray Guachoa gets caught and this coup is overturned before more and more people are hurt by it.'

Switching off the flashlight, Doug prayed that the Lord would lead Troy and Jack safely back to base and that they might be able to alert the loyal officials and police in time to prevent the movement of the drugs and the use of those weapons they had now discovered. Marcia prayed for the people of Ecuatina, especially the young people. She asked God to save them from the misery of heroin and crack and bring them to faith in Christ.

The two of them closed the trap-door and covered it with the waste paper once again. They had barely finished their task when they heard the sound of an approaching car.

'Quick! This way,' said Doug, leading Marcia to a large stack of paper sacks at the back wall quite near to the sliding door. As they waited they heard the car doors slammed, followed by voices talking excitedly, even angrily. The sliding door opened noisily to allow the men entry and soon the warehouse was a blaze of light.

From their hiding place Doug and Marcia could see Guachoa and two of his henchmen. It was difficult to make out what they were saying, but it was obvious they were very angry and very nervous. Things were not going well with the attempted coup. Guachoa strode towards the pile of waste paper and began to throw the bundles of reject sacks out of his way until the trap-door was clear. Lifting the trap-door he brought out about a dozen rifles, together with ammunition. His henchmen produced sacks into which they put the weapons. Then, closing the trap-door and replacing the bundles of waste,

Guachoa led the men back towards the sliding door.

'Presidente,' cried one of the men, stopping in his tracks and pointing to one side. 'Presidente, look.' Gauchoa turned impatiently, but what he saw filled him with even more anger and panic than ever.

To his horror Doug realised that the rebels had discovered the stillage of sacks which had burst when Marcia bumped into it, spilling the heroin. Gauchoa ranted on at the two men, clearly assuming one of them had carelessly damaged the bags of dope.

Suddenly the rebel leader became quiet. Stooping down he picked up something he had noticed on the floor.

'What a pity we overlooked the spilt heroin in the dark,' whispered Marcia. 'What's that he's got in his hand?'

Doug stretched his neck out as far as he dared to see what Gauchoa was doing. Finally he turned to Marcia. 'I think it's a small book of some kind. Obviously something we didn't see when we were looking about.'

Marcia's eyes widened with disbelief. 'Oh no,' she said. 'My notebook. I remember now. I was carrying it when I bumped into that stillage. I must have dropped it.'

'Is your name in it?' asked Doug.

'Yes,' she answered. 'I'm afraid it is.'

They were interrupted by Gauchoa's furious tones. There were no two persons who had done more to wreck his uprising than these two foreigners, Doug and Marcia. Now he saw that one of them, perhaps both of them had been there that very evening. Had been – and perhaps still were there in the warehouse which was his evil headquarters. Motioning to his henchmen to spread out, Guachoa led the search for his enemies.

CAUGHT

Doug prayed quietly. He asked God's forgiveness for the waves of anger and irritation with Marcia which were washing over his mind. Hadn't he told her it would be dangerous? If only she'd stayed at home there would have been no notebook to alert the rebels, and no torn sacks to arouse suspicion. Of course, Doug had to admit that without Marcia they would never have discovered the drugs.

'Lord, give us a way out,' prayed Doug quietly. 'Surely you haven't brought us all this way to perish at the hands of these crooks. Have you not said, "I am with you and will rescue you."'

Suddenly an idea came to Doug and turning to Marcia he whispered it briefly.

'I'll make my way quietly to the far side of the warehouse, then I'll attract their attention and draw them after me so that you can slip out the door. Once outside, get out of Pampalla as fast as you can – back to Juan Pedro's – and over the border.'

It was a brave sacrifice – one facing certain death to let another live, but to his horror Doug found Marcia wouldn't budge.

'It's my notebook – it's me they'll expect to find here. Besides if I hadn't torn the sacks they wouldn't have know we were here because they wouldn't have seen the heroin.'

'Will you please do as I say?' pleaded Doug, choking back feelings of anger. He would probably die for this woman, and that was hard enough, but to think she wasn't even going to take the chance to escape. It was too much.

'Why don't you go, Doug? After all they don't know you're here. It's me they'll be expecting to find and...' Her whisper faded into a half-embarrassed, half-amused silence as Doug looked at her in mystified disbelief. Without another word he shook his head and turned gloomily to wait for the seemingly inevitable.

Gauchoa's henchmen were almost upon them. Doug recognised one of them as the small friend of Scarface Carlos who had guarded him when he had been held captive in the warehouse.

The other man was Mr. Santara, the clerk whom Lieutenant Vidal had known. He certainly didn't look much like a clerk at that moment as he carried his menacing rifle. The men were only a few metres from Doug and Marcia. All at once a shout rang out. It was Gauchoa calling to his men. Whatever he said didn't meet with their instant approval and he had to shout at them again.

Doug could hear them grumbling amongst themselves as they moved away toward the door. Was Guachoa leaving? No, he was continuing his search with increased diligence. The men must have been sent to bring others to speed up that search and flush out the unwelcome intruders. If only Gauchoa knew how close he had been.

If Doug thought the immediate danger was past, however, he was in for a rude awakening.

'A ... aa ... choo! Aa ... a ... choo!' Marcia's eyes were streaming. The sacks behind which they had been hiding were covered with dust and Marcia had finally succumbed in her long struggle to hold back a sneeze. She looked so miserable and apologetic, Doug couldn't help feeling sorry for her, notwithstanding the danger they were in.

'Come out! Come out at once,' barked Gauchoa.

'You stand up slowly,' whispered Doug, 'I'll try to circle round behind him.'

Timidly the American girl rose to her feet.

'Ah! Our friend, the reporter,' sneered the rebel leader. 'I believe you have lost something – a notebook. Come and get it.'

'Y... you can keep it – if you want,' stumbled Marcia. Gauchoa's narrowed eyes were full of bitterness and anger.

'But for you and your British friend I would have taken over this country easily. Now, I am having to fight for it. If I lose I may well lose my life. What do you think I am going to do with you and your friend?'

Marcia knew, but she couldn't bear to answer. She felt her knees go weak and her heart pounding. The evil man raised his rifle to his shoulder.

'Gauchoa – over here.'

It was Doug shouting from somewhere to the man's left. Turning he fired a volley of murderous shots. Marcia screamed and ran to where she had heard Doug's voice come from, but he was hiding behind a pillar. Gauchoa's bullets were bouncing off the pillar and flying into the sacks piled high on their stillages. Doug could see heroin pouring from one of the bullet holes.

Catching a glimpse of Marcia as she ran, the crazed football President fired at her also, but again the sacks absorbed the bullets. Marcia wanted to wake up as if from a nightmare. Could this really be happening? Was she really dodging death like this? Bravely, Doug sprinted between the piles of paper sacks and from pillar to pillar drawing Gauchoa's fire. He hoped that both he and Marcia would be able to edge nearer and nearer to the door until finally they could make a dash for freedom.

The plan seemed to be working well until a freak accident happened. As Marcia ran behind a large stack, one of Gauchoa's bullets dislodged an unsteady bundle of sacks on top of the stack. It fell, catching Marcia a glancing blow on the head, and knocking her off her feet. As she struggled to get up Gauchoa raised his rifle to kill her. Doug was too far away to tackle the rebel leader, but he dashed over to Marcia and took her in his arms, using his body to shield her from the assassin's bullet.

A single shot rang out. Doug felt his body tense up. A rifle clattered to the ground and the sound of moaning could be heard. It took the friends a few moments to realise that it wasn't themselves who had just been shot but Gauchoa.

'Are you two all right?' asked a familiar voice.

'Jack,' they replied together. 'But we weren't expecting you back for hours. How did you make it?'

'Well, when we got back to Juan Pedro's we realised it didn't require two of us to go and get help, and that you were in real danger here. So I headed back as quickly as I could. By the look of things I didn't get here any too early.'

Jack turned to the stricken rebel whom he had wounded in the arm.

'So you are Gauchoa the Great! Well, your reign is over. Your people have been routed in the south, and they're hemmed in on the east. The loyal people are calling for your overthrow and President Mendez will be back in power by morning.'

The traitor glowered at his captor.

'You won't take me alive. I still have men loyal to me and they'll be back here anytime. I will decide about your future, instead of you deciding about mine.'

'That's right!' gasped Marcia. 'We'd forgotten about them.'

'I wouldn't worry about them,' smiled Jack. 'During the last hour there's been a big demonstration in the main street. I even saw policemen and soldiers in the crowd and they were calling for President Mendez to be brought back.'

Turning to the sullen Gauchoa he said, 'I don't think you'll see your friends again until you see them in jail. Once we've tied you up we're taking you to police headquarters, and that will be the end of your rebellion.'

Gauchoa struggled, but with his wound he was no match for Jack who soon had him trussed up like a turkey. Bundling him into the car he had parked outside, Jack drove them all round to police headquarters, being careful to put out the lights of the warehouse and close the door.

At police headquarters, order was being restored out of confusion and corruption. Lieutenant Vidal and certain other officers had been placed under arrest and their replacements were taking over. Although many senior officers had been implicated in the coup, the Chief of Police, a man called Fernando, had been loyal to President Mendez.

Fernando was overjoyed to see that Guachoa had been captured, and he had him put in jail.

'We will bring the television cameras at once. The people of Ecuatina must know that the traitor is in custody.'

When Jack explained about the drugs and guns hidden in the warehouse Fernando insisted on accompanying the drug officers personally.

As Jack, Doug and Marcia were driven through he streets in Chief Fernando's limousine they could see crowds of delighted citizens and soldiers celebrating the overthrow of Gauchoa's plans. Marcia felt like pinching herself to see if she was really there experiencing this amazing sequence of events – being shot at one moment and driven in a stylish automobile the next. What would here editor think back at *The Manhattan Echo*?

Fernando shook his head sadly as he saw the huge quantity of drugs concealed in the paper sacks. The experienced men of the drug squad identified a mark on each stack which contained bags of drugs, and this aided their search. They would, in time, examine all the sacks in the factory. A British reporter approached Doug together with a television camera man.

'Two weeks ago you told us how you were held captive by Gauchoa's gang and how you had escaped. Obviously, the information you provided alerted the authorities and forced the rebels to make their move before they were properly ready. Can you tell us what happened after that?'

Doug answered as fully and carefully as possible, and pointed out to the cameraman the vault of guns and ammunition which Jack had revealed to Fernando. The Police Chief's eyes looked as if they would pop out of his head with amazement.

'He must have planned to kill a lot of people,' said Marcia, pointing to the drugs being removed by the police. It was a great moment for freedom.

Marcia looked round to see where Doug had gone. He was standing quietly, away from the glare of the cameras and she sensed immediately that he was praying, giving thanks for God's deliverance.

She realised that if Jack had arrived one minute later at the warehouse he would have been too late to save Doug and herself. God's timing was perfect. She thanked him too for all he was doing in their lives. She had learned so much so quickly, and with every lesson, she felt humbled and grateful.

'The World Cup is having to take second place in the country's news right now,' Marcia observed, looking at the large number of cameras and reporters crowding into the warehouse.

Doug jerked his head round to look at her. 'Do you know this, I'd forgotten all about the World Cup during these last few days, and that's what I came out here for.'

Doug wondered how the squad were coping with all the pressure. It was hard enough competing at this level without having an uprising to contend with. A smile came to his lips and widened into a grin.

'What's the joke?' asked Marcia.

'I'm just thinking about Bill Cheyne. I wonder who he's shouting at now.'

They both laughed. The Scotland manager liked everything 'canny' as he used to put it – not too many disturbances, no rocking of the boat. Well, it certainly hadn't been like that in Ecuatina! Yet Bill had been such a good friend to them in these difficult days.

Doug snorted.

'What's up now?' asked Marcia.

'I'm thinking of Bill again,' he replied, 'coaxing Mrs. Keir to give you that funny anorak and trousers.'

They both laughed. All the pent up tension of the past few days exploded in giggles of suppressed mirth. They both felt so silly, laughing till the tears rolled down their faces.

'Do you think ...' laughed Marcia, 'do you think Gauchoa's laughing?'

'I doubt it,' answered Doug, 'but that cameraman looks very pleased with the picture he's getting of you.'

Marcia straightened up immediately, wiping the tears from her eyes only to find there was no camera focused on her at all, and she could laugh freely again.

'I'm glad you two are enjoying yourselves.'

It was none other than Bill Cheyne who had hurried down to the warehouse when he saw Doug and Marcia on television.

'We've been worried sick, about you both. I'm going to ask the police chief if we can take you back to our hotel for a meal. You must be ravenous. You could stay with us as a guest, Marcia. I'll ask Mrs. Keir if she has any clothes she can loan you for the next few hours. Mackay, what are you laughing at? I suppose you think Marcia won't be our guest very long as we'll soon be heading home after defeat by Ecuatina. Well, we've got other ideas about that. We still think we can win. After all one of our young players has turned up again after a week of starting fires and dodging bullets.'

There was a twinkle in Bill Cheyne's eye. It was good to see them both safe and well.

'I don't know if I'm fit to play,' said Doug, 'but I'm certainly keen.'

'Once you've had a rest you'll feel better,' said Bill Cheyne. 'We don't kick off until 3.30 p.m. You can spend about an hour loosening up in the morning. I'll decide tomorrow whether to put you on from the start, or use you as a substitute. This is an important game for us. If we lose it's another massive disappointment, if we win we could go all the way to the final.'

'How are the squad?' asked Doug. 'Have we any injuries?'

'None,' replied Bill Cheyne. 'If you pass fit tomorrow we have all twenty-two players to choose from. So we have no excuses. We really need to do well.'

Doug was silent as he watched the police taking away drugs and guns. How unimportant football seemed at that moment. The future of a nation had hung in the balance. The welfare of hundreds of thousands of young people had been seriously at risk. The World Cup had been completely overshadowed as this drama had been acted out, and Doug and Marcia had been right in the middle of it.

When he had doubted his own fitness for the match, it had been his emotional fitness that Doug had been thinking of. Yet it was to play football he had come to Ecuatina – to play for Scotland. As he thought once more of the enormous privilege this was, Doug quietly prayed that he might be fit in every way to do his best for his own land as he had done his best for this small Latin American country in which he now found himself.

STAR OF HONOUR

The glare of the equatorial sun greeted the players of Ecuatina and Scotland as they emerged from the tunnel on to the field of Pampalla Stadium. A huge roar reminded the players that the Stadium was full, mainly with fiercely patriotic Ecuatina supporters. The collapse of the coup, and the growing awareness of what they had been saved from, stirred the volatile South Americans to boiling point.

It was the sun, however, which worried the Scots most, and the absence of any breeze whatsoever. Doug, who was playing from the start, had been given a brief work-out that morning. Bill Cheyne had intended to test him for an hour, but had called him in after thirty minutes. 'I can see you're fit enough,' Bill had said, 'and you'll exhaust yourself in this heat.

Keep your energy for the afternoon.'
Doug had been glad go get inside for a
cold shower.

The teams lined up for the National
Anthems. In a few minutes the whistle
would blow and Scotland would be
playing in one of the most important
and most demanding matches in their
long history. Doug was surprised to see
President Mendez appear. He wore the
uniform of his office, including a hat
with a magnificent plume in it. He was
introduced to both teams, the Scots first,
then his own country. Doug received a
particularly warm handshake from the
President as he passed along the line.

Having greeted both teams President
Mendez made his way to the centre of the
field where a small stage had been quickly
set in place. His appearance had been
greeted with tumultuous applause, which
had continued throughout the inspection
of the teams. Now, as he mounted the
few steps, the crowd chanted his name,
demonstrating the popular support he
enjoyed.

Calling for silence, he began to speak.
He thanked the people for their support
and pledged that, with their help, he
would seek to lead the nation to greater
strength and unity. He reminded them
of the very real dangers they had faced

from the ambitions of Gauchoa, and issued a public warning to any other would-be rebels that the people of Ecuatina would reject them as certainly as they had rejected Gauchoa.

President Mendez had been speaking in Spanish, with an interpreter translating into English, for the benefit not only of the Scots, but the world press.

'We as a nation,' he went on, 'owe a great debt to a young man here on the field this afternoon, who discovered and exposed the treacherous plot against us. He risked his life not once, but three times to alert us to our danger.'

Senor Mendez outlined what Doug had done and concluded by saying, 'We in Ecuatina have an award for civil bravery – The Star of Honour. I can think of no-one worthier to receive this award than our friend – Doug Mackay.'

With that he beckoned an embarrassed Doug to come forward. There was thunderous and sustained applause. When it had died down, Senor Mendez said, 'You have served us well. Surely God brought you here for more than football. We will always be indebted to you. With this award we confer upon you the further honour of Liege-Man of Ecuatina, which entitles you to free travel to and from our country at any time. You will never again have to pay for anything in Ecuatina.'

Doug was overwhelmed. He stuttered his thanks and made to rejoin his team-mates, but President Mendez restrained him.

'Doug Mackay has been a hero in our midst, but he has not been alone. We also have a heroine whose bravery and wisdom has brought us political support when we need it most. She too has earned The Star of Honour. This is Doug's sweetheart from America – Miss Marcia Holman.'

The crowd roared its approval, as Marcia came forward to receive her award from the President. Doug felt slightly sick, there was no other word for it. This moment was being shared by millions of people the world over and while it had been embarrassing enough to have a medal hung round your neck, it was positively humiliating to hear Marcia and himself described as 'sweethearts'. Doug could see the smirks on his team-mates' faces who obviously thought they had been missing out on something.

President Mendez wasn't finished, however. Putting one arm round Marcia's shoulder and the other round Doug's shoulder, he said, 'We give you both our best wishes. Remember, when you are married you can live at no expense here in our country. We would love to have you.' As Doug returned to his place in the team he felt emotionally drained.

'Aye, boy, some dark horse you are,' muttered Ally McTaggart with a grin. 'Incidentally, I hope you're immune from tackles with that medal on.'

Doug had forgotten The Star of Honour. Hurrying to the touchline he handed it to Bill Cheyne. Once again Doug received a huge ovation. He looked up and for a moment he was looking into the eyes of Marcia, who was waiting to go up into the Presidential Box to sit with Senor Mendez and the other dignitaries. She smiled gently as if she knew the discomfort he was feeling, a discomfort not because he was ashamed of her in any way, but because he was too private ever to enjoy having his life and feelings held up to public scrutiny.

Marcia's smile seemed to say something else. 'I'm with you. I want you to do well – and I know you will.' As he went back for the kickoff Doug prayed quietly and thanked God that he had restored calm and confidence to him through Marcia, at the very moment when his own shyness had tempted him to resent her as the cause of his embarrassment.

At last the game was underway. Any thought Doug had of being treated specially by the Ecuatina players was quickly dispelled, for as he ran the ball down the right wing he was charged into touch. Minutes later his heels were clicked as he sped past an opponent, and the first time he jumped to head the ball he got an elbow in the face. One other Scottish player was having a particularly rough time – Ally McTaggart. Ecuatina had decided these were the key players and they must be kept out of the match – at all costs.

'These boys must all be second cousins of your pal, Gauchoa,' panted Ally to Doug as they waited for the keeper to take a goal-kick. Doug grimaced as he rubbed a recently hacked shin.

'They seem to be content to keep us from scoring. They've hardly mounted an attack,' he said.

'They don't need to,' answered Ally. 'A draw at the end of ninety minutes would suit them. Extra time would be too much for us in this heat.'

'Then we had better stick in a goal soon,' said Doug with determination. 'Look,' he added, 'Martin's getting a lot of space out on the right. If we give him the ball and make ourselves available in the penalty box something might come of it.'

The goal-kick reached the halfway line where Ron Macleod, Doug's Dalkirk Albion team-mate, headed it in the direction of Ally McTaggart. He barely had time to control the ball when an Ecuatina player closed him down. Ally had just passed the ball to Doug when the defender crashed into him. Doug had already checked that Martin Skinner was clear on the right and he immediately sent a quick pass along the ground to him.

Skinner took off at speed, hurdling the clumsy tackle of the fullback. Reaching the edge of the penalty box he squared the ball into the path of Doug who was coming up at speed. Ecuatina's captain tensed himself for one last desperate lunging tackle on the Scot, but just at that instant Doug jumped over the ball letting it through to Jim Bremner who hit it hard and low into the net.

The pleasure of the Scots was dampened by the sight of Ally McTaggart lying in pain in the centre circle. He had been felled by a vicious tackle and had to leave the field on a stretcher with a badly bruised leg. The Latin Americans were shaken by the goal and couldn't get back into the match before half-time.

'You've really got them going,' urged Bill Cheyne as the players flopped wearily in the pavilion. 'Just hold on to the ball, keep possession, and they'll get frustrated.'

'Hmm!' moaned Jim Bremner, holding a throbbing ankle. 'If you ask me they're frustrated enough.'

'We're getting no protection from that referee,' grumbled Geordie Neilson. 'He's ignored one late tackle after another.'

'They're trying to rattle you, lads,' soothed Cheyne. 'Keep cool and keep probing for another goal that would tie it all up for us. Remember, you beat Brazil and this team isn't a patch on Brazil.'

As the Scots emerged on to the pitch for the second half they were greeted with boos and whistles from the huge crowd. Ecuatina, by contrast, received a tremendous welcome as their fans tried to life them and inspire them to victory.

The Latin Americans quickly showed that they could play positive and constructive football and Scotland were pinned back in their own half. They were missing Ally McTaggart's steadying influence and, increasingly, they were feeling the heat. The pressure was bound to tell.

Ironically, although the Scottish defence had refused to stoop to tackles employed by their opponents, the goal they lost was the result of a penalty given for Geordie Neilson's challenge on Santos, the home side's striker. It wasn't an easy decision to understand considering some of the tackles Ecuatina had got away with and the yellow card was shown to Neilson for protesting too vehemently. The pressure on Santos was enormous as he stepped to take the kick, but he was an experienced player and he gave Bill Hamilton no chance.

The crowd became almost ecstatic, knowing that with only five minutes to go, the game could well go into extra time which would stretch the weary visitors to breaking point. It was to Ecuatina's advantage to get the game bogged down in midfield till the ninety minutes were up, and they were doing it to good effect. Then Doug saw one last chance to win the game as the ball rolled out of play at the halfway line.

One of the Scottish substitutes was Billy Williamson who could on occasion summon up a long throw-in. Shouting to him, Doug sprinted down-field. He was over thirty yards away when Williamson released the ball, which fell about ten yards behind Doug.

The Ecuatina right-back went forward to collect it but he hadn't counted on the hardness of the sunbaked pitch. The ball bounced high over the defender's head and landed perfectly for Doug who steadied himself and fired a high dropping shot for goal. The goalkeeper was quite unprepared for this. He made a brave attempt to stop the shot but even as he jumped the sun's glare distracted him and the ball ended up in the net behind him.

The crowd fell silent, the players' heads went down. The soccer dream was over, just as the political nightmare was over, and the minister's son from Dalkirk had played a part in ending both.

There were celebrations in the visitors' dressing room at the end. They were tired, very tired, but they were happy. Now they could rest until the quarterfinal tie, the draw for which was to be made that very night. There were no easy teams to be paired with and, in the event, Scotland had to play Germany. It was a tough draw, but at least they had four days before the match was to be played. That night the Scots were able to relax back in their hotel and reflect on the fact that whatever happened now they had made a major impact on the World Cup. They had let nobody down.

The one big disappointment was the injury to Ally McTaggart. He would be out for at least a week and would miss the game with Germany. Doug did what he could to cheer him up. He liked Ally and had learned a lot from him as a player, but he was in for a surprise that night as he sat on the edge of Ally's bed chatting about the game.

'What's it all about?' asked Ally in his usual direct way.

'What's what?' responded Doug.

'Life. Religion. What is it all about? I'm no mug, I can see there's something different about you. You're a very ordinary bloke and yet things happen around you all the time. There's something, and I can't figure out what it is.'

'It's not something,' answered Doug, 'it's someone. My folks have brought me up to know the Lord Jesus as my Saviour, and I am learning increasingly as I get older to trust in the Lord. Jesus once said to his first disciples, "Have faith in God!" Well, Ally, I take that as the motto for my life and I find God to be with me all the time – in my studies, football, leisure time, adventures, if that's what you call them, as well as in church. God is the someone who makes the difference in my life. Does that answer your question?'

Ally nodded silently.

'Now let me ask you a question. Would your life be better or worse if you trusted God like that?'

Ally said nothing for a long time. When at last he spoke his words were full of meaning.

'I don't think I could live like that. I believe God is there, but I don't have the faith you have. God seems a long way off.'

Doug was praying as he listened. Then he said, 'The question is, "Do you want to know God?"' He went on, 'The Bible tells us about a man who once came to Jesus in great need of his help. When the Lord told him that all things are possible to him who believes, the man replied, "Lord, I believe, help my unbelief!" It was all so new for him and he really needed Christ to work in his life, meeting those deep needs. You need Christ like that, Ally, and he is there to help you as he helps me, and to answer your prayers as he answers mine. At first it can be difficult, but as you find him answering your prayers and steering your life in a certain direction faith becomes easier and more natural.'

They talked together for a while and Doug shared passages from the Bible with Ally and told him about his own experience. As he settled down to sleep that night Doug thanked God for another day of blessings – The Star of Honour, Marcia's smile of encouragement, the game with Ecuatina, and most of all, the talk with his roommate.

DAYS OF DECISION

Doug usually enjoyed training for he saw it as an investment in his own fitness for everything he had to do, be it physical, mental or spiritual: he didn't like to be sluggish or out of condition. Things were weighing on his mind, however, and he was finding it hard to concentrate. There was a general air of unease about the Scottish camp, as if they were a team who had advanced in the competition to a level they could not handle.

Their performances had been fitful, depending on the form of a few players, rather than the clicking together of the whole team. In the quarterfinal tie the Germans would quickly expose and exploit any weaknesses, unless Scotland could seize the game by the scruff of the neck, so to speak, and force the opposition back on their heels.

It was something else, however, that was troubling Doug. In two days' time Marcia would be flying home and both of them knew they had things to talk about before she went. Doug remembered their last discussion, how abruptly it had ended and how painful it had been. Most of all, he remembered how difficult it had been for them to talk and think rationally when they had both been so involved emotionally. That evening they were to have dinner in a small hotel in a quiet part of town, then go for a walk by the riverside.

The afternoon passed, painfully slowly, but at last the time came for them both to leave the team headquarters and travel by taxi across Pampalla. Marcia looked lovelier than ever and the happiness of her growing faith shone through in all she said. They recalled the many adventures they had enjoyed in the few short weeks they had been together and marvelled at how God had caused their paths to cross in this tiny, but lovely, South American country. As they finished the meal and relaxed with a coffee Doug at last plucked up courage and began.

'I'll miss you very much when you go, Marcia. It's funny how strong affections can become in so short a time. When we talked seriously at Juan Pedro's I tried to say something to you which I felt very deeply about, but I know I failed then. It's very difficult to make sense at times like these but maybe you can help me. What I was trying to say was that the only right reason for going with a girl is that you are meant to marry her.'

'But how can you know whether you are meant to marry someone,' interrupted Marcia, her voice betraying the exasperation she felt. 'Surely you have to go together for a time before you can be certain, one way or the other.'

Doug was silent for a moment. 'The way I see it, as Christian young people we have all our lives before us and because these lives belong to God we need his help in all the decisions we have to make, especially the big ones, such as the career we're going to follow, and the person we're going to marry. We need to ask God to guide us to make the right choice. Especially we need to ask him to make sure we don't make the wrong choice.'

Marcia nodded, 'I agree. It would be hopeless to end up training for the wrong career and spending your life trying to fit into a job that just isn't made for you. Naturally, it would be even worse to be married to the wrong person. You would never be really happy until you went to heaven.'

As Marcia said these words she shuddered, for the very thought of being unhappily married repelled her. But she quickly went on, 'The thing I can't see is how this can happen when you know you love someone and think about things the same way they do, when you want to be with that person and share your life with him.'

'Maybe, the truth is,' answered Doug, 'that there has to be not only the right person, but also the right time. Personally, I've always believed that the question of career has to be settled before the question of marriage. If I am to marry someone then I will be responsible for providing for her and for any family we may have. If I don't have a job or career it's going to be very difficult to fulfil that responsibility. That's why I want to finish my degree, because by then I might have a clearer idea of what my life's work is meant to be.'

'But that will be another year at least, maybe two,' argued Marcia. 'And surely it's a bit old fashioned to speak about the husband as the provider! I certainly don't need any man to provide for me; in fact I could provide for you until you finish your studies. You are a bit old fashioned and set in your ways. You can't expect women to be retiring wallflowers with no independence of their own.'

'You may well be right,' he answered. 'But if I'm set in my ways I think they are the ways of the Bible. I certainly don't have much time for the new ideas about marriage that are just confusing the roles of men and women. I believe we have different but equal parts to play, like the singers in a choir. Soprano and tenor are different but equal. After all, didn't God say to the first wife, "Your desire will be for your husband and he will rule over you"? The husband has the harder role and if his wife is going to fight with him and insist on getting her own way all the time he will never be able to fulfil it.'

Doug was firm but his voice was not angry. He felt calm and assured as he went on, 'Before I met you, Marcia, I always sensed I would probably be single at least till my late twenties so that I could cope with being a man and finding God's direction for my life before I took on the responsibilities of marriage. Having talked to you again tonight I am more sure than ever that I've been right. Love is not just a good feeling that comes when you are with someone attractive, it's a decision to be with someone and care for that person for the rest of your life. It is a decision of the mind as well as the heart and it requires a lot of maturity. I enjoy being with you very much, but I'm not ready to make that commitment yet – to any girl.'

With those words Doug had given Marcia up. He had grown to like her immensely for she was a most pleasant girl, but at that moment he knew so clearly that he loved God far more than Marcia. God's will was all important and as Doug followed that divine will the Lord would not withhold any good thing from him. He felt a great sense of relief and liberty. It was as if Christ's Lordship over his life had been challenged and had triumphed in the end.

Marcia turned to look at him, but there was neither contempt nor irritation in her eyes. 'I want God's way too. I..I just don't know the Bible well enough yet and, even more, though I'm sure you're right and I'm wrong, the truth is I'm afraid – afraid I'll lose you. If you go back to Scotland you could end up marrying somebody else, and what would happen to me then?'

'But Marcia, you've got to learn to trust God. I pray regularly about who I will marry, or what my career will be. Do you think God will let me make a mistake when I trust him? Neither will he let you make a mistake as you trust him. You don't need to worry or be afraid. After all, it's no accident we met here. Surely God meant us to come to know each other and feel deeply for each other. We can trust him to work things out for the future.

'For my part, I'm certainly not going back home to look for a girlfriend, but to get on with living my Christian life. You said that I'm old fashioned and maybe I have to plead guilty to that charge because I believe God has one person chosen out to be the marriage partner of another and he will bring them together in his time. As long as we wait on God he will bring each of us to the right person. Adam didn't have to go looking for Eve, God brought her to him.'

Marcia brightened, as if a dawn of understanding was stealing across her mind. In her own way she was rather old fashioned, set in the pattern she had inherited from her parents. She had not, until that moment, really thought that a girl could leave something like marriage up to God. Surely there must be room for a bit of female manipulation to influence male decision-making, and because she had thought like that she had feared Doug might be making excuses,

131

and that she might be facing rejection
again as she had faced it throughout
her childhood. Now, at last, she was
beginning to realise that the answer to
this fear of being left 'on the shelf' was
simple straightforward trust in her loving
heavenly Father.

'Are you suggesting that we go
our separate ways and wait to see if
God brings us together again?' asked
Marcia.

'I think that's the best idea,' answered
Doug. 'Each of us has a lot of growing
to do spiritually before we're ready for
marriage and in the meantime we can
be serving God singly, you in journalism,
me doing my studies.'

'And we can write to each other,' said
Marcia.

Doug was so relieved that all had
worked out well. He had feared he would
lose Marcia altogether, but his trust in God
had been vindicated and she had come
to see things as he did. Now, with this
matter happily resolved as far as it could
be, he could concentrate on the match
with Germany.

It was hard saying 'Goodbye' to Marcia
at the airport and for the rest of that day
Doug felt strangely lonely, almost as if an
important part had gone out of his life.
He could never have expected to feel so

attached to the girl when he first saw her in the reporter's room following the victory over Brazil.

For all his honest spirituality and clarity of understanding he had to admit he missed her and it was a relief later that afternoon to slip into the local church he had attended in Pampalla and sit quietly in prayer, handing his future over to God. As he sat there the words of the twenty-third psalm came into his mind, 'The Lord is my shepherd, I shall not want.'

It seemed to Doug as if God was saying, 'Let me lead you and I will give you what is best. Whatever you must give up I will more than make up.'

* * * * * * * * * * * * * *

The floodlit stadium was well filled as Germany kicked off against Scotland. The blistering heat of the day had given way to a comfortable evening temperature in which the players of both sides could give of their best. The early exchanges were even as the game flowed from end to end. Scottish hopes rose as first Skinner, then Bremner went close with attempts at goal, while at the other end only the brilliance of keeper Hamilton kept the Germans at bay.

With the interval approaching and both sides locked together an error in the

Scottish defence let their opponents in to grab a half-time lead. Ken Wilson, the sweeper, turned to send a pass back to Hamilton, but he hadn't noticed Geordie Neilson, the central defender, who had moved almost directly into the path of the ball, which cannoned off him and ran to Ruhl, the clever striker from Munich, who pounced and slammed the ball into the net.

The Scots came out for the second-half determined to pull back that goal, but instead they quickly lost another. Germany were playing with confidence and a skilful passing movement broke down the Scottish defence to allow Gerhardt to score number two.

Things looked bleak for Scotland, but they fought back and Martin Skinner linked with Ron Macleod on the right to set up an easy chance for Andy Macdonald, a striker who was getting his first cap following an injury to a more experienced player. Macdonald made no mistake from close range and the game was wide open once again.

Up to this point Doug had played with his usual skill and composure without getting into a scoring position. But as the game drifted into its closing stages and the action slowed down he was able to run on to a pass from right-back Young and send a high curling right-foot shot over the head of the advancing keeper for the equaliser. From there till the end of the ninety minutes neither team could seize the initiative and normal time finished with the teams still even.

Bill Cheyne encouraged his players as they waited for extra time to begin. 'You're doing well. Don't lose heart. You're giving them a lot of problems, especially with the close-passing, and they were becoming increasingly frustrated as you kept possession of the ball in the last twenty minutes. You might easily have won. Keep playing as you've been doing. Ron and Doug, you keep forcing the pay forward. We just need one break to make it into the Semi-Finals.'

The two teams returned to the fray, each determined to grab the opening goal as quickly as possible. Each half lasted fifteen minutes and during the first spell the Scots came under heavy pressure again and again. In the second spell of extra time the game remained as tight and close as before with neither side seeming able to gain an advantage over the other. Then at last a break came for Scotland.

It was Ron Macleod who started the move when he intercepted a long pass out of the German defence. Quickly he transferred the ball to Pete Macdougall on the left wing. Pete sent the fullback one way and moved the other way to open up the defence and swing the ball over for Andy Macdonald to head it towards goal. The youngster was getting ready to jump with delight when the header rebounded off the German goalkeeper's right-hand post back into play. Before the defence could move, however, a player in a navy-blue shirt threw himself at the loose ball and knocked it over the line for the winning goal.

'Well played, Doug,' shouted Bill Cheyne, jumping with excitement from the dugout. 'We've done it. They won't catch us now.'

Bill Cheyne was right. Doug's late goal proved to be the winner and his team trooped (or rather staggered) off the field to the prolonged applause of their fans, not one of whom was regretting for a moment the long journey they had made to Ecuatina.

LETTER FROM AMERICA

'Horace Buchan! Your folks must have heard from you at last. Derek Gallacher! That's a bulky package – maybe it's a pair of shooting boots.'

Bill Cheyne was handing out the mail to his players and enjoying the banter that went with it.

'What about me, boss?' moaned Don Dickson.

'No, your pension book isn't here,' replied the manager, to hoots of laughter. 'That's all, folks.'

Then with a twinkle in his eye he added, 'There is one letter here ... but I don't think it can really be for any of you lot. The address is written in a beautiful female hand and there's a definite scent of lavender.' The players, who had been turning away to talk amongst themselves, were all ears.

'Now what name is this? Who is this highly favoured gentleman?' Various humorous suggestions were hurled at him by the players, but Bill kept up the drama till the end, announcing in a voice that called forth applause, 'Why, it is Mr. Douglas Mackay.'

The embarrassment Doug felt as the jeering and catcalling were directed at him was far outweighed by the relief at the arrival of the letter from Marcia. It had been nearly a week since she had flown home to New York, and each day had seemed like a week in passing.

It was only now that she was gone that Doug realised how fond he had become of her. Marcia had plenty to say in her letter, all of it interesting. In the first place, she had been able to have a long chat with Troy and Jack on the flight home. The secretive nature of their work made it difficult for them to open up and say what was on their minds, but they had unburdened themselves to Marcia, admitting that they felt God had been at work in Ecuatina overturning Gauchoa's wicked plans. They also sensed that God wanted to relate to people personally as he was doing for both Marcia and Doug.

'The one thing I cannot get clear,' Jack had said, 'is whether this is for everybody or just for some special people. I hear about people seeing the light as they put it, but I don't know too many who have seen it.'

Marcia had explained that far from waiting for something to happen, it is up to us to seek God as he has commanded us. She had quoted a passage she had been reading in the Book of Isaiah which pointed out that the wicked should "turn to the Lord and he will have mercy on him, and to our God, for he will freely pardon".

Troy and Jack had asked her to suggest churches they might attend in their local areas and, at first, Marcia had been struggling to think how she could direct them when each lived so far away from her. Then she had remembered Doug's answer to her when she had asked the same advice for herself.

'Jesus Christ is your Lord. He will guide you as you trust him. Pray that he will not let you miss his place for you.' That was how he had put it to her. In similar vein she had encouraged the Texan and the man from Chicago to prove just how great God is by asking him to lead each of them to the right place of worship. Marcia had been thrilled a few days later to receive a phone call from Troy informing her that his uncle was a keen Christian and had arranged to take Troy along to church with him.

Another piece of news that was much less thrilling was the reception Marcia had had from her parents. Both her mother and father had been delighted by their daughter's meteoric rise to fame, as nightly news bulletins had carried film and story from Ecuatina, but as the full significance of her conversion finally broke on them they became impatient and angry.

'Do you mean to say you want to marry a preacher, or be a foreign missionary? Don't you realise there's no money in that kind of life?' Her mother had spent hours trying to change Marcia's mind, but all to no avail. It was her father's reaction that troubled her most, however, for he had withdrawn into a sort of pained silence, as if Marcia had somehow rejected him by becoming a Christian. She had very wisely, but humbly, spoken to her father about this, pointing out that though she could no longer accept his values she still cared for him.

Marcia had gone to the Lutheran Church to which her family belonged. The minister had come to the area only a few months previously and she had found his first sermon really helpful.

Being Marcia she had got talking to the minister after the service and ended up inviting him round to their home, a decision that had sent her mother into a flap and driven her father even more into his shell. Marcia was learning quickly that not everyone enjoyed a minister's visit.

Naturally, she wanted to know all about Doug and how his preparations for the next World Cup match were coming along. (She was becoming quite a soccer fan.) Marcia also wanted to know if Doug could come to America directly the World Cup was over. All expenses would be paid, courtesy of *The Manhattan Echo*, as the editor was very keen to interview him and feature his story in the paper.

The idea interested Doug, but it would have to wait. Right now he had other things on his mind. In little more than twenty-four hours Scotland would take to the field against the brilliant South American team, Argentina, who were now confidently expected to win the competition. The mood in the Scottish camp was one of grim determination. Having come this far they were not going to give up without a struggle, even although injuries had weakened the side and limited manager Bill Cheyne's final selection.

Offside in Ecuatina

Ally McTaggart was improving, but his leg injury would not be completely healed in time. Keeper Bill Hamilton was also unable to play. He had sustained a nasty wrist injury in training and his place would go to Don Dickson. Ironically, Dickson had been the number one choice as goalkeeper when the competition started but when food poisoning ruled him out of the match with Brazil, Hamilton had taken over and made the position his own. Now, it was Don's turn again. There were also niggling injuries troubling Ron Macleod and Martin Skinner, but these were small and not expected to keep them out of the team.

There was something else on Doug's mind. He had always believed Scotland were good enough to go the whole way and win the World Cup. They had their strong points as had the other teams in the competition and if they could concentrate on these points and take the initiative from the opposition they could beat them. Already Brazil and Germany had found that out to their cost. The thing that was beginning to trouble Doug was that the nearer they came to the Cup Final the nearer they came to Sunday football, for the World Cup Final was traditionally staged on a Sunday.

It wasn't that he had any doubts on the matter. Sunday being the Lord's Day, it was quite wrong to use it for playing football. Doug saw clearly that underlying the lame excuses for Sunday sport was a disregard for God's will and he would not go along with that. He felt sorry for those who could see nothing special in that day that was set aside for worship, learning, Christian fellowship and rest, and it grieved him to see the growth of Sunday sport and entertainment in Britain. How sad it would be if the day was ever reached when the times of Christian services and celebrations on the Lord's Day were dictated by the growing demands of Sunday leisure and sport.

No, there was no doubt in Doug's mind about this matter of playing in a Sunday Cup Final. The question rising in his mind was one that related to the Semi-Final. If he was picked to play he obviously could not do less than his very best, but suppose that helped put Scotland in the Final, would he not have played his part in forcing his fellow team-members to play on Sunday?

Doug concluded that what his team-mates did about the Cup Final was up to them. For his part, he was happy to play football on a Wednesday evening and, if selected, he would play in the Semi-Final. As far as the Final was concerned he had made his position clear to Bill Cheyne right from the beginning.

Doug was chosen for the Semi-Final and the Scots fielded the strongest side they had available. Earlier that day there had been a real shock in the other Semi-Final when Nigeria, one of the emerging soccer nations had beaten the more fancied Russians in a classic match. Bujong, Nigeria's brilliant striker had scored twice in their 3-2 win. Could Scotland make it a day of surprises for the experts by toppling Argentina?

The Scots started well, moving the ball easily from player to player and three times one of their forwards had a gilt-edged chance to open the scoring. Perhaps at last the occasion was getting to them, for each time the chance was squandered. These misses not only discouraged Scottish players, they stirred the Argentinians to push forward in search of a goal for themselves and as the first half drew to a close only the brilliance of Don Dickson in goal kept the score-sheet blank.

It was obvious that the South American team were treating their opponents with great respect for they were marking them closely and keeping the play tight rather than dribbling with the ball or swinging long adventurous passes from side to side of the field. The second half started as the first half had finished, with both teams still sizing each other up.

Then Scotland took the lead with a strange goal. Doug, back defending during an Argentinian attack, cleared a shot off the goal line with his goalkeeper well beaten. Following the ball up he hit it to Horace Buchan and looked for an open space to get the return pass.

Doug vaguely noticed that the South American players seemed to be protesting angrily about something to the Spanish referee, but as he hadn't heard the whistle he just kept on running with the ball. Quickly he reached the halfway line without being tackled and, seeing Derek Gallacher clear on the left wing he sent an inch-perfect pass for him to run on to.

Hardly had the ball left Doug's foot when he received a hefty challenge from behind. Had the Argentinian player connected properly with Doug's leg the injury could have been serious but as it was, the impact forced the boot off his foot. Picking himself up, Doug ran on towards the opposing penalty area, much to the annoyance of his opponent who had brought him down, who was

145

obviously hoping to force Doug to retaliate and thus get himself into trouble with the referee.

The young Scot hobbled forward in time to see a great shot by Gallacher rebound from a post and be knocked away by a defender. The ball was coming straight toward Doug – to his bootless right foot. With two defenders bearing down on him Doug hit the ball as hard as his stockinged-foot would allow. It wasn't nearly hard enough, nor straight enough, and the ball would have run harmlessly past the post for a goal-kick, had the Argentinian right-back not tried to clear it. In doing so he miscued completely and hammered the ball into his own net.

As Doug left the celebrating ranks of Scottish players to look for his missing boot, he noticed the referee being besieged by furious South Americans.

'They thought the ball had crossed our line before you cleared it,' said Ron Macleod to Doug.

'Not at all,' replied the youngster, 'I was standing on the line when I kicked it out. They should learn to play to the whistle.'

The referee finally had to caution two Argentinian players, showing them the yellow card, before he could get the match restarted. Back came the South Americans, combining skill with determination in their quest for the equaliser. The Scottish defence held firm until the last minute of the game when Argentina scored the goal their all-out attacking play richly merited. This pushed the game into extra time, with fifteen minutes each way to be played.

There was little to choose between the teams as the minutes ticked away, except that the South Americans were coping better with the heat. Don Dickson was playing brilliantly and with only five minutes to go he tipped a net-bound shot round the post for a corner, which was scrambled away by Geordie Neilson.

Martin Skinner collected the ball on the edge of his own penalty area and set off at speed down the right wing. Having come on as a substitute nearly ten minutes from the end of normal time Martin was fitter than most of the other players on the field and his pace carried him past two opponents before they could tackle him.

Seeing Martin approaching the halfway line, Doug summoned all his reserves of energy and sprinted into the Argentine half of the field. Had the young winger released the ball quickly a scoring chance could have been set up, but he delayed too

long and Doug found himself in an offside
position, caught between Argentina's
goalkeeper on the one side and the
defenders on the other.

As Doug looked up he saw Martin losing
the ball to the left-back who began to
move upfield to start a counter-attack.
Tired as he was Doug began to jog
towards his own half of the field. Then for
no apparent reason, the Argentinian left-
back turned and sent a long pass-back
to his keeper. The effect of this was to put
Doug technically in an onside position
and, without waiting to fathom out the
mystery of this soccer gift the Scot sprinted
to collect the loose ball.

The keeper, frustration written all over
his face, was coming off his goal-line
quickly in a desperate bid to narrow
Doug's angle for the shot. However, it
was something else that flashed through
his mind in those seconds – a goal
now could mean a Cup Final place for
Scotland, and a giant headache for Doug
as controversy raged round his stand on
Sunday soccer.

CONVICTIONS ARE COSTLY

It was the easiest of scoring chances, even given the tense atmosphere of a World Cup Semi-Final and the lad from Dalkirk made no mistake, chipping the ball over the advancing keeper's head so that it bounced into the empty net.

The stadium erupted. Increasing numbers of Scots had been coming to Ecuatina with each success their team had in the competition. There were fully twenty-five thousand of them in Pampalla that night and they cheered the team to the echo. As the final whistle blew Doug was lifted shoulder high by his team-mates, who obviously believed he had played a vital part in the game.

'That was excellent, lads,' said Bill Cheyne once the team had returned to the dressing room. 'You've earned your place in the Final. It will be a great day for Scotland if we can bring that Cup home with us – and, somehow, I don't think we'll ever have a better chance.' As the dressing-room celebrations went on the manager moved quietly over to Doug.

'Son,' he said, putting a hand on his shoulder, 'you've had some frightening experiences since we came to Ecuatina but it will all be worth it when we lift that Cup. You played well tonight. I just hope Ally McTaggart will be fit to partner you and Ron in the midfield. That's where the game will be won or lost.'

Doug looked at him with widening eyes. 'Surely you haven't forgotten what I said before we left Scotland, Mr. Cheyne,' said Doug.

But Bill Cheyne's puzzled look told him that indeed the manager had forgotten.

'I don't play football on Sundays.'

'But, but, Doug, this is the World Cup Final. This is the big one.'

'What good is it for a man to gain the whole world, yet forfeit his soul?' quoted Doug. 'I don't want to disappoint you, Mr. Cheyne, but I'm not playing a match on Sunday, not even this one.'

That evening a knock came to Doug's hotel room door. His roommate, Ally McTaggart was downstairs in the lounge relaxing with the other members of the team. When Doug opened the door he found Mr. Keir and Bill Cheyne together with two other officials of the Scottish Football Association. The young player welcomed them in and once they were seated Mr. Keir began to speak.

'Bill has told us about your problem, lad, and we will do all we can to help you. We've already sent an official request to FIFA headquarters for the date of the Final to be changed to Monday.'

Coughing nervously, Mr. Keir went on, 'We are doing all we can for you; we look to you to do your best for us. Can we take it that if FIFA refuse to shift the match from Sunday that you will honour your commitment to your country?'

Doug shook his head. 'I told Mr. Cheyne when he selected me that I would not play on a Sunday. That was my commitment to God and I fully intend to honour it.'

'But Doug,' interrupted Maurice Smith, the SFA Vice-President, 'you're playing really well. If you are not in the team the pattern of play may be seriously affected.'

'Mr. Smith,' replied Doug, 'for me to play would be wrong and I know it. Have you any idea how badly a man can play with a guilty conscience?'

The conversation went on for some time but at last the officials realised they could not hope to change Doug's mind. They must hope instead that the date could be changed, although there was little likelihood of that happening. FIFA had arranged the dates well in advance and there had been no hint of opposition to their proposals at the time. As far as the organisers were concerned this was an internal problem for the Scots to sort out.

As news of Doug's decision leaked out the first reaction of players, fans and the press was one of near disbelief. But that disbelief quickly turned to irritation and then to outright anger. The Scottish press especially tried to put pressure on the young star to change his mind. Doug was accused of lacking patriotic feeling and of displaying selfishness and irresponsibility.

Dark rumours began to circulate that he had fallen out with the manager over the amount of money he was to be paid for appearing in the Final, which was ridiculous since he was an amateur and received no money at all for playing football. Wisely, Doug didn't even bother to answer these wild allegations. He knew that the men who made them were really resentful towards God for using this situation to speak to them and remind them that they too were responsible to him for how they lived. These men did not want their consciences to be disturbed.

Each day brought increased pressure for Doug to change his mind, although not from Bill Cheyne or the other officials who had accepted FIFA's decision that the game must go ahead on the Sunday. They respected their player's integrity and knew it was pointless to pester him. Not so the fans. Letters poured into the hotel and the telephone switchboard was jammed with calls – all with one message – Doug must play.

In addition to this the whole atmosphere in Pampalla was becoming increasingly electric as thousands of Scottish fans arrived for the final. It was like an invasion. Accommodation resources were stretched to the limit and the airlines could hardly cope with increased demand for charter flights.

Two things happened which greatly encouraged Doug at this point. On the Friday before the Final President Mendez made a public appeal to FIFA to reschedule the match. Not only Ecuatina, but the other nations owed a debt to Doug for exposing the attempted coup by the drugs baron Gauchoa. Therefore, reasoned President Mendez, this was a special case. After all, what possible difference could it make to FIFA if the match were played on Monday rather than Sunday. The organisers still felt they couldn't give way and insisted the match go ahead as planned.

The other incident, however, made a big impact on all concerned with the competition. That same Friday evening Doug had a visit from none other than Samuel Bujong, Nigeria's top goal scorer. Along with Doug he had been voted best player in the Cup competition so far.

'I've come to tell you that I too am a Christian,' began Bujong. 'Until now I never gave much thought to playing football on the Lords's day, but I can see you are right. We should not be doing this. I have told my manager that, like you, I will not be playing on Sunday. He is not happy, I'm afraid, and Samuel Bujong is not a popular name in Nigeria right now. But then, our Lord Jesus was not always popular either.'

Doug embraced his new found friend. It was such an encouragement to find someone else helped by his own example, and especially a great player like this. The Nigerian officials were not as sympathetic to Samuel as the Scots had been to Doug and the striker was sent home on a flight from Pampalla the next morning.

At last the significance of all this was getting through to the FIFA officials. It might be too late to change things this time, but a press release indicated that, in future years, the date of the Final would be sufficiently flexible to take account of the scruples of conscience which individual players might have. Provided players gave notice to FIFA when chosen to represent their nation in the World Cup, that nation would not be required to play the Cup Final on a day unacceptable to that player or players. It was a great step forward, and it ensured that the showpiece of soccer would not be spoiled again by the loss of players like Mackay and Bujong.

Doug was delighted. He was so glad he had taken a stand for principle. Yet he felt deeply the cost he had had to pay. It was bad enough having to miss the greatest match he could ever hope to play in, it was even worse to be lied about, condemned and misrepresented.

'It's a strange thing,' he said to Ally McTaggart.

'What's strange?' replied his roommate.

'This offside business.'

'Eh?'

'I mean it applies to life as well as football, don't you see?' said Doug.

'I'm not sure I do,' replied McTaggart.

'Well, I may be wrong but it seems to me I've been offside in so many ways since I came to Ecuatina. First, there was the boy stealing my camera, then Guachoa got hold of me. There was Marcia and the emotional problems she brought. Now I miss the World Cup Final. It's as if I've been in the wrong place all the time.'

'Funny you should say that,' replied Ally. 'I've had to do a lot of thinking in the last week, being injured like this, and I've thought about you quite a bit. Didn't you get your place in this squad because of the way you sprung the offside trap at Wembley?

'And wasn't it your escape from Gauchoa's warehouse and your meeting with Marcia which saved the country from that coup? Even the goal that got us into this Cup Final – you were yards offside before the fullback played you back into the game with his crazy pass-back. Each time it's worked out for the best.'

Ally's words shook Doug. Here was an onlooker seeing what, for the moment, he himself had lost sight of. How often Doug had read the words of Romans 8:26, "All things work together for good to those who love God." Yet, for the moment, he had pushed them to the back of his mind and was concentrating on the hard knocks he had taken. Yet, all Ally said was true, for each set-back had proved in time to be a springboard. Would he yet beat this one remaining offside trap and play in the World Cup Final?

'Another thing you need to remember, Doug,' Ally went on, 'is that you have made a decision to miss this game. I haven't. I didn't get a choice – only a big kick on the leg. I can't play even if I want to. The physio told me that I couldn't take the chance for at least four days. And remember, football is my life – my religion, if you want – although I admit you've made me rethink my priorities quite a bit. Do you think I don't long to have the chance to make a decision about playing on Sunday? Do you think I haven't prayed about it and longed to be there? But it's out of my hands.'

It was a moment of special insight for Doug. Christian convictions were costly, but it was a wonderful privilege to be free to pay that cost and know God would make it up in his own perfect time.

THE STORM

As Ally and Doug were talking a knock came to the door. It was Bill Cheyne.

'I came to check for the last time whether or not you feel you can play on Sunday. I won't try to force you, naturally, but I think I should warn you there seems to be a lot of bad feeling building up back home as well as here in Ecuatina amongst the fans who have travelled for the game. They don't understand why you won't play.'

Doug shook his head. 'I can't do it,' he said. 'I'd rather be rejected by people for doing the right thing than be popular for doing wrong.'

Bill Cheyne nodded, 'I knew that would be your answer, but I had to ask. Now I can finalise the team selection and get ahead with planning our tactics.'

Before he turned in for the night Doug prayed that God would bring good out of this problem: 'Thank you, Lord, that Christians won't have to face this dilemma in the future. But, even yet, you are able to work things out for this year. Help me to be faithful to your teaching in the Bible, whatever happens.'

On the Saturday there was a short letter from Marcia, (only four pages) encouraging him to keep trusting the Lord, as young people everywhere were being challenged by his faith and principles.

'I know it can't be easy for you,' she wrote, 'but God will look after you through it all. Then you can return home knowing you have honoured the Lord in every way.'

These words were a great encouragement to Doug as he endured the unpleasantness of so many spiteful and nasty comments which he received in the mail.

Sunday dawned bright and clear. There was a quiet tension at the breakfast table in their hotel as the Scottish squad looked ahead to the game. The morning dragged by for most of them, although Doug made his way to church as he had done each Sunday morning since coming to Ecuatina.

The preacher was speaking about the temptations which came to Jesus Christ in the wilderness and how he resisted them by obeying what the Bible taught and by trusting fully in God, his heavenly Father. The sermon helped Doug tremendously for he missed his father's daily support which would have been readily forthcoming had he been at home. As it was he had received a letter from his father which he had read and re-read many times.

By the time Doug returned to the hotel the squad had already left for the stadium. He had a quiet lunch and then went up to his room to read. Soon, to his surprise he had to put the light on as dark clouds rolled over the city.

Meanwhile, at the stadium, the teams were already standing to attention while the National Anthem of each nation was played. The black clouds released a heavy shower of rain which pelted the players mercilessly as the Nigerian Anthem was being played. When the band struck up the Scottish Anthem the downpour turned into a thunderstorm with flashes of lightning tearing angrily through the dark clouds and noisy peals of thunder rumbling ominously overhead.

All at once there was a resounding crack as lightning struck one of the goalposts breaking it in two. Bandsmen, players and officials sprinted for cover as the storm intensified. There could be no play until the goalpost was replaced and that would be impossible until the storm abated.

The minutes ticked past and as the torrential rain left pools of water all over the ground, FIFA officials realised that if this lasted much longer the match would have to be postponed. An announcement was made to the crowd that if the storm was still raging in fifteen minutes time, there would be no alternative but to abandon any attempt to play it that day.

The next fifteen minutes saw no improvement whatsoever. The storm had not blown itself out. The organisers reluctantly announced the game was to be postponed for over forty-eight hours to give the pitch time to dry out. As each person left the stadium they would receive a counterfoil which would admit them to the match on Tuesday evening. A half-smile played on the lips of Bill Cheyne as his players changed in the dressing-room to return to their hotel.

'Well, well, Peter,' he said to Mr. Keir, 'there was no way we could persuade FIFA to move this match from Sunday, but someone else has been far more persuasive than we could be.'

'Yes,' grinned Peter Keir, 'I think Doug will be very happy with today's result.'

'Mind you he will have to be content with a place on the substitutes' bench,' said Bill firmly. 'I must keep faith in with the eleven men I chose to start the game. I too have principles.'

'I know who else we can have on the substitutes' bench on Tuesday evening,' added Peter Keir with sudden enthusiasm.

'Who?' asked the manager.

'Ally McTaggart. The doctor said four days would do for his leg injury – and that's up on Tuesday.'

'I'd forgotten,' said Bill, a grin brightening his features. 'We could have the pair of them on again.' This news was a confidence-booster to the whole squad as they returned to their hotel.

Doug was amazed when he heard the account of what had happened. He had realised the players would be up against it playing through a raging storm, but any thought of the match being cancelled hadn't come into his mind.

He was happy, really happy, to have the chance to appear in a World Cup Final even as a substitute. But he was also delighted for Ally. The biggest disappointment for Scotland had been the injury to their best player and now that he could play in the Final, even for a short time, was a bonus for the whole team.

'God really does answer prayer,' said Ally. 'It seemed so impossible that I would ever make it, but because you stuck to your beliefs, Doug, the game has been put back two days and I get a chance.'

Only the lightest training programme followed on Monday, while on Tuesday the manger talked with the players, going over tactics they had practised in training. At last the great moment arrived and the teams stepped out on to the turf of Pampalla Stadium.

The ground was dry, the goalpost renewed, and there was no sign to suggest that only two days before a storm had battered the place. The National Anthems over, the teams lined up and with a blast of the referee's whistle the Cup Final was under way. By far the larger part of the crowd had come from Scotland. There were lion rampants, kilts and bonnets everywhere, but right from the start it was the Nigerian fans who were having the most to shout about.

The African team's skilful left winger, Obuna, was putting Rory MacAlpine through the mill with darting runs and clever footwork that opened up repeated chances for his team. Obuna's crosses and passes into the penalty box were simply asking to be struck into the net, but Nigeria were paying a heavy price for having sent Bujong home so quickly. They had no other striker of his class to finish the moves being set up.

Scotland, for their part, were weak in the midfield area – normally their strongest. Ron Macleod was striving hard to get the team going but they were missing Ally and Doug madly. At last the inevitable happened. Obuna, seeing his strikers were wasting every pass he gave them, decided to cut inside and have a go for himself. His shooting was as good as his dribbling and he gave Don Dickson no chance with a right foot shot from ten yards.

At the interval Bill Cheyne tried desperately to lift the spirits of this team. He made a few tactical changes, but these were powerless against the quick-moving Africans who had used the interval to better tactical advantage and were now stretching the Scottish defence by attacking down both wings. Still, the missed chances kept Scotland in the game.

Then, midway through the second half, they went further behind. Obuna, twisting and turning, had poor MacAlpine so totally confused that, more by accident than anything else, the fullback obstructed the Nigerian in the penalty-box, causing him to fall. The penalty was given and the Nigerian captain, Ankda, gave Don Dickson no chance from the spot.

A great wave of despair swept over the Scottish fans. Their team hadn't even began to play and the game was nearly over. But suddenly a roar of anticipation began to sweep the stadium.

Scotland were making a double substitution – Strang and McWilliams were going off, and McTaggart and Mackay were coming on. Almost at once there was a difference, for the two newcomers closed down the Nigerian midfield cutting off the supply of ball to Obuna and the forwards. Instead, Scotland now had the ball and were determined to use it to full advantage.

Martin Skinner and Pete MacDougall who had hardly seen a pass until now came more and more into the game, and it was a foul on Skinner that gave Scotland a great scoring chance.

The winger was wriggling through the Nigerian defence when he was upended right on the edge of the penalty box. There were roars of anger from the Scottish fans who felt sure a penalty should have been given, but the decision of the Brazilian referee had been accurate. The offence had occurred just outside the box.

Doug picked up the ball and placed it. Then turning round he called to Rory MacAlpine, urging him to come up and take the kick. The right-back hurried forward, but just as the Nigerian defence were relaxing Doug turned and quickly thumped a fierce shot over the heads of the defenders who were forming a wall of defence against the free-kick. Not only did Doug's quick thinking catch the Nigerians napping, but the shot was high enough to clear the defensive wall and low enough to go into the net off the underside of the crossbar.

The goal shook the Nigerians who found themselves forced back on to a defensive type of game they were not used to. A neat inter-passing move between Macleod, McTaggart and Buchan let Jim Bremner through. His right-foot drive beat the keeper, only to bounce back off the post. Quick as a flash, Doug charged in to hit the rebound through the keeper's leg into the corner of the net.

The crowd went frantic with delight. From seeing their team all but beaten they were now witnessing a fight-back that had put Scotland on the threshold of victory.

Singing and dancing filled the stadium and a sense of anticipation swept the crowd as they realised the sudden turn of events had shaken Nigeria's confidence, forcing them to realise they were now no nearer to victory than they had been when they kicked off. The full weight of those missed chances was beginning to weigh on their shoulders.

The African side restarted the game with only about two minutes to go and set up an attack that nearly produced the winner. Obuna's cross eluded keeper Dickson, but the player at whose feet it fell sliced it past for a goal-kick. The Nigerian manager buried his head in his hands. If only he had recalled Bujong, even after Sunday's match had been cancelled. But now it was too late.

As the game entered its last minute Dickson's goal-kick was headed over the halfway line by Ally McTaggart to Pete MacDougall. Ally was limping already. His leg had not quite healed and he would be a virtual passenger if extra time was required.

Pete MacDougall passed inside to Bremner who was tackled and beaten by Ankda. The big Nigerian strode forward only to be dispossessed by Doug who sent the ball quickly back to MacDougall. Pete tricked the fullback and bore down on the goal. As the keeper came toward him, Pete passed it to Doug who was striding in on goal. Ankda had followed him all the way and lunged at him in a desperate effort to prevent the goal.

Cries of 'Penalty' rose from fifty thousand throats, but as Doug crashed to the ground he heard no whistle – for the referee had been perfectly positioned once again – to see a limping figure in a dark blue jersey take advantage of the loose ball to side-foot it into the net. Ally McTaggart had not only played for Scotland, he won them the World Cup.

As Doug lay on the ground watching the ball hit the net and seeing the crowd rise as one man to acclaim the winning goal, he thanked the Lord who had made it possible for him to be a part of it all. The words from the Bible – 'Those who honour me I will honour, says the Lord' – came to his mind and he was so glad he had stood by his beliefs.

Ally McTaggart had disappeared under a team of delirious players who could hardly grasp what had happened. He emerged smiling broadly and grabbed his roommate in a bear-hug. 'We made it Doug, we made it. It paid to do it God's way.'

As the World Cup was presented to Geordie Neilson the crowd went wild, as if half a century of frustrated hopes had at last been realised. So many soccer disappointments could now be forgotten for they had won the World Cup, the first European side to win it on South American soil, and they had done it in style.

Doug looked at the waving mass of flags and scarves, and listened to the incessant din which accompanied their lap of honour. What a moment! What a month! Images flashed before his mind – Wembley, Ecuatina Airport, the opening ceremony, Gauchoa, the warehouse, the winning goal against Brazil which silenced the samba drums, the Mendez family and the burning barn, the stillness of his hotel room that stormy Sunday – and now this amazing experience.

There was one image that wove its way in and out amongst the others – the loveliness of a girl's smile – Marcia. She would be watching at this moment. How was this friendship going to work out? The years to come would answer as God led each of them in the way that was best, but for the moment, almost involuntarily, Doug looked up into the camera that was tracking the team in their lap of honour and raising his hand, he blew a kiss. He hoped she had seen it just as he hoped he would see her again one day.

'Lord, your ways are marvellous,' he prayed in his heart. 'We can trust you for the future as surely as we have trusted you in the past. With you all things are possible.'

Other books by Cliff Rennie

Goal behind the Curtain

Doug Mackay proudly represents his country at football in a land in turmoil both on and off the pitch. He has to use his speed to get past border guards as well as opposition defences. But the biggest threat seems to come from within his team.

ISBN: 978-1-87167-647-1

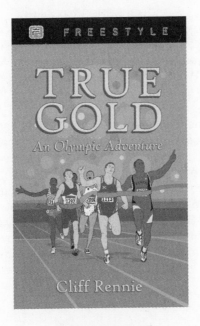

True Gold

The huge Olympic stadium in London is full
of cheering spectators. The competitors are
under starter's orders. Everyone holds their
breath - and they're off. One runner's life hangs
in the balance. There is only one way that he
can survive, and it's up to Jason to find it. This
is a thrilling tale of adventure and excitement.

ISBN: 978-1-84550-655-1

The Adventures Series
An ideal series to collect

Have you ever wanted to visit the rainforest? Have you ever longed to sail down the Amazon river? Would you just love to go on Safari in Africa? Well these books can help you imagine that you are actually there.

Pioneer missionaries retell their amazing adventures and encounters with animals and nature. In the Amazon you will discover tree frogs, piranha fish and electric eels. In the Rainforest you will be amazed at the armadillo and the toucan. In the blistering heat of the African Savannah you will come across lions and elephants and hyenas. And you will discover how God is at work in these amazing environments.

Rainforest Adventures by Horace Banner
ISBN 978-1-85792-627-9

CHRISTIAN FOCUS PUBLICATIONS

Christian Focus | Christian Heritage | CF4K | Mentor

Christian Focus Publications publishes books for adults and children under its four main imprints: Christian Focus, Christian Heritage, CF4K and Mentor. Our books reflect that God's word is reliable and Jesus is the way to know him, and live for ever with him.

Our children's publication list includes a Sunday school curriculum that covers pre-school to early teens; puzzle and activity books. We also publish personal and family devotional titles, biographies and inspirational stories that children will love.

If you are looking for quality Bible teaching for children then we have an excellent range of Bible story and age specific theological books.

From pre-school to teenage fiction, we have it covered!

Find us at our web page:
www.christianfocus.com

CF4•K
Because you're never
too young to know Jesus